Lock Down Publications and Ca$h
Presents

I0658200

OPPS
CRY TOO

Blood on the Streets

Written By
SAYNOMORE

First Edition 2025

Printed in the United States of America

This is a work of fiction. Names, characters, places, and incidents either are products of the author's imagination or are used fictitiously. Any similarity to actual events or locales or persons, living or dead, is entirely coincidental.

Lock Down Publications
P.O. Box 944
Stockbridge, GA 30281
www.lockdownpublications.com

Like our page on Facebook: Lock Down Publications
www.facebook.com/lockdownpublications.ldp

Stay Connected with Us!

Text **LOCKDOWN** to 22828 to stay up-to-date with new releases, sneak peaks, contests and more…

Like our page on Facebook:
Lock Down Publications

Join Lock Down Publications/The New Era Reading Group

Visit our website:
www.lockdownpublications.com

Follow us on Instagram:
Lock Down Publications

Email Us: We want to hear from you!

PROLOGUE

"I knew you was going to fuck that bitch last night. Word to my mother, I saw how she was looking at you," Ray-J told KP as they were walking into the store.

"Bro, I fucked the shit out that bitch raw-back, and had her sucking my dick 'til I bust all in her mouth. That's not even the crazy part, Ray-J."

"So, tell me then, nigga. What the fuck you leave out?"

"This bitch was sucking my dick when her man called. She put him on speaker and all. She told her dude she was at her home girl house, while she licking and sucking all over my dick. I'm busting in her mouth, she telling him she eating. That shit was bananas last night."

"I knew shorty was a freak. Bro, what the fuck we getting out of this store?"

"Just get me some chips and a soda. I'm late as fuck. I was supposed to been dropped this bag off. You know I'm hot as fuck right now."

Ray-J placed the chips and soda on the counter along with a box of Dutch's and Newport's. After paying for everything, they walked out the store.

"You know what I wanted to tell you, KP? That nigga Jagger was talking crazy about you last night, saying you owe him a check or some bullshit like that."

"Bro, fuck that nigga. Real talk. We was rolling dice about 2 weeks ago and I broke that nigga pockets. He wanted to run the game back. I dubbed that shit out and walked off."

"Yeah, he was in his bag about that shit, for real-for real."

"That nigga will get over that shit; hands down."

Before Ray-J could say a word, Jagger walked up to them with his hand behind his back. "What's up, nigga? You thought shit was sweet with me?"

"Nigga, you pulling up on me like my heart pumps Kool Aid. Nigga, you got me fucked up. Take your L and call it a day, nigga."

"No, you got the game fucked up, pussy." Jagger pulled his gun out and pointed it at KP's face.

"This Cash shit. Man, you asking for a death wish."

"I don't give a fuck. Fuck that nigga Cash, and he can die, too."

"I ain't coming off of shit. Do what the fuck your heart telling you to do."

"Have it your way, then." Jagger pulled the trigger, shooting KP 3 times in the chest, killing him. He then pointed the gun at Ray-J as he took the bookbag off KP. "Keep this shit in the streets, nigga. You know how to find me."

Ray-J watched as Jagger took off running down the block. He walked up to KP's dead body and looked at him as he had blood bubbles coming out of his mouth, dead to the world. When Jagger killed KP, Ray-J knew it was going to be a long, bloody Summer. Cash wasn't going to let this shit ride.

Jagger was a dead man walking. He just opened the devil's playground, and many more bodies were going to drop before the Summer was out. Cash didn't play. He was going to show that opps cry, too.

Chapter 1

"What we got here, detective?" Detective Cross asked as Detective Moore was bent down, looking over the dead body.

"His name is Kevin Smith, AKA KP. Shot three times in the chest," Detective Moore said as he was standing up, pulling a cigarette out of his pocket.

"What street gang is he a part of?"

"From the tattoos on his right arm, the letters B.D.B. That stand for Buggie Down Browns. He's from Albany Avenue and Smith Street. Cash is the big dog over there, and you know what Browns stand for, right?"

"Yeah, Detective Moore. *'Believe real ones will never snitch'*."

"Yeah, that's one of them, but it also stands for *'Bullets run out with nasty sounds'*. So, Detective Cross, get ready to hear the nasty sounds because Cash ain't about to let this go unanswered. Somebody just opened up pandora's box."

"Who you think had enough heart to take one of Cash's guys out? And still be in the city?"

"We will find out real soon, because the next 187 we are called to is going to be a retaliation murder. So, get ready for a hot summer, and a large body count."

Detective Cross looked at the body one more time before walking off.

"Detective Cross, so what we need now?"

"A good supply of body bags."

***

"Cash, Ray-J is in the other room. He said he needs to talk to you about some shit that went down last night."

Cash looked through the center window from the kitchen at Ray-J standing there. Ray-J looked at Cash looking at him. Cash was a different type of animal. A murderer. A real killer. He'd been putting in work for so long. He's one of the only niggas from the east coast that the west coast respect as a triple OG. He didn't give a fuck who you were; his bullets don't have no names on them. The tattoo on his neck on the left side— ABK— stood for *anybody killer*, and he stood on that shit.

Cash leaned over and told B-God in his ear, "Bring him to the basement. I'll be there in a minute."

B-God nodded his head and walked off. "Yeah, he told me to tell you y'all going to talk in the basement. There's too many ears up here right now."

Ray-J ain't say nothing he just followed B-God to the basement. A few minutes later, Ray-J saw the light from the basement door open and Cash walked downstairs smoking a blunt. He was wearing a white beater, black jeans with Timberland boots and a fitted cap.

"Ray-J, I know why you are here. I know what the fuck you want to talk about. My question is what took you so long to get to the fucking house to let me know the little homie got rolled last night?"

"I was trying to let shit calm down last night. I ain't want to bring no heat to the house."

Cash pulled his blunt and looked at Ray-J as he blew the smoke out his mouth and grilled him. "Look you going to get a walking pass, but everything comes with a price. You was there when the little homie got rolled and you let this fuck nigga take a half of brick of my shit. Find this nigga Tigger. I don't give a fuck where he is at. When you see him, you better paint the walls, the inside of his car, the street sidewalk. I don't give a fuck but paint it with his blood. If the police is there, guess what nigga crash out!"

"I got you, Cash."

"Good. Now go handle your business, little homie."

Ray-J went to walk off when Cash placed his hand on his shoulder and said,

"So much depends on our reputation. We kill niggas because we guard it with our lives."

Ray-J nodded and walked off.

Chapter 2

Tigger sniffed two lines of cocaine as he sat at the table, thinking about how he should have killed Ray-J's bitch ass. He was about to make another line when there was a knock at his front door. He picked his gun up to see who was at the door.

He yelled out, "Who the fuck is it?"

A voice yelled back with anger in its tone. "It's Gangstar, nigga. Open the fucking door. Showtime's with me too."

Tigger put his gun in his waist band and opened the door, looking at Gangstar and Showtime as they walked in his door.

"It's 9am, y'all banging on the door like y'all the police."

"Nigga you better be glad that we ain't the fucking police. Word on the block, you flatlined that nigga KP from Browns," Showtime said.

"Man fuck that dead body. He tried me like a bitch, so I pulled up rocked that baby to sleep. I took that nigga bag with a half of bird inside. You know how the fuck I get down"

"You know 9 out of 10 times that's Cash shit you took. You know he's going to want blood, on GP for that."

"Man fuck that nigga. Cash bleed just like the rest of us. If them niggas want smoke, let's give them what they asking for then."

"Just be ready Tigger, because shit going to get dark real soon and we need to hit them niggas first and hard. You get what I'm saying?" Gangstar said.

"Yeah, I'll get the shit done. You don't have to worry about that. I know where that nigga be at, homie."

"Just know with Cash you only get one shot, and he don't be alone."

"I already know."

"Now, if the hood is going to war over you, it's time to pay your dues. You got a half of bird.

I need half of that half, homie."

"It's over there on the table, Gangstar."

Showtime walked to the table and broke the half of brick in half, bagged it up and walked back over to Gangstar.

"Yo Tigger, stay dangerous. The heat is on."

"Copy that, Gangstar."

Showtime dapped Tigger up before walking out of the apartment.

Gangstar stopped and looked at him. "Stop playing with your fucking nose and get on point!"

***

"Sometimes you have to be the bad guy and do what other motherfuckers won't, no matter how much pain it brings to a family. So if you have to, you can call me the bad guy."

Freestyle looked at Cash, knowing his heart had no boundaries when it came to the streets and the game he played so well. "So, who going to eat the plate? Because them go-gettas ain't just going to lay down. Gangstar ain't no hoe, and he don't give a fuck about who is around when it's time to pop the bottle."

"Gangstar cold suck a dick sideways. If that nigga step out of line, we are going to take that nigga head off. Fuck Gangstar! Look, I need to go take care of some business. Watch the block. I'm out."

"Say less, homie." Cash dapped Freestyle up before walking off.

***

S-B sat on the hood of the car smoking a Black & Mild as he waited for Big Apple to be released from the county jail. Big Apple been locked up for 18 months for aggravated assault, and possession of a weapon.

That's when S-B saw the county jail doors open and Big Apple walked out of them, throwing up Browns as he walked to the car. S-B got off the hood of the car and gave him a pound, followed up by a hug.

"How it feel to be out, nigga?"

"It feels good to be free, and out that hell hole. So, what's been going on on the block?"

"You remember the little homie KP?" S-B said as he walked to the driver side of the car and got in. He looked at Big Apple as he got into the car.

"Yeah, I remember the homie, a little pretty ass nigga fucking all the bitches in the hood."

"Yeah, that was the little nigga, word. Baby boy got rolled a few days ago. He got hit for a half of brick."

"Yo, stop playing. Who the fuck did that goofy shit and these niggas still breathing?"

"Shit is wicked out here, but you know Cash put that spring cleaning list out. You know he ain't going for that shit."

"Already, look bro, I ain't trying to be in these streets naked. I need a tool."

S-B smiled, reached, opened the glove box and pulled out a Glock-9.

"I already had you in mind before I picked you up, bro. It's fully loaded, and she clean."

Big Apple looked at the gun in his hand and smiled. "Not for long. I'm about to put a graveyard on this bitch. Take me to go see Cash."

"We are already on our way there," S-B said as he smiled and nodded his head.

Chapter 3

"Killer B, what's the word? What the fuck you got going on?" Tigger asked him as he was looking around the party.

"Fucking these bitches and make this money but fuck all that. What's this I hear you caught that 187 on one of them Browns niggas?"

"You already know how I get down but I'm about to go get a 40 and roll some dice. I'll get at you later."

"Say less, my nigga." Tigger walked over to Money as he was rolling the dice talking shit to everyone when Gangstar walked up behind him.

"Tigger, you take care of that business yet?" Tigger turned around and looked at Gangstar."

"I'm roll that nigga. I just ain't been seeing him around."

"It's hard to find a nigga when you smoking weed and ready to roll dice."

"That nigga will be taking his last breath real soon, fam."

"Say less then. Just stand on your business, homie." Gangstar patted him on the back before walking off.

***

S-B watched everyone smoking, laughing and talking shit to everyone at the party, as he smoked his blunt talking to Ray-J.

"Big Apple is home, so the streets are about to get real dangerous. Cash and Big Apple together is like the devil and a demon side by side. Real talk, little homie, if you don't body this nigga Tigger tonight, your name is going to be on that grocery list. I fucks with you. That's why I'm out here with you tonight," SB said as he passed Ray-J the blunt.

"That nigga is going to take his last breath tonight, on Browns bro."

"Good, make sure it's loud and messy."

"Already." Ray-J cocked back his M16 he was holding with the drum on it. He pulled the blunt, looking out the window of the black SUV he was sitting in. He was waiting on his moment to fire off.

***

Tigger looked around. It was 12am as he started to walk out of the party, when Tina and Rock walked up to him.

"Nigga, you bouncing already?"

"Bro I'm lit right now. I'm about to head to the spot but what you and beautiful about to get into?"

"I don't even know bro, but we damn sure not about to call it a night."

"Yeah, Tigger, we might end up on 42nd Street."

Tina was bad. She was a real dime piece with a banging body, dark skin, long jet-black hair. She kept her name clean in the streets. Everyone wanted to get with her but she curved them all. She wasn't a jump off, period.

"Fuck it. I'll ride out with y'all. We on 42nd Street."

"That's what the fuck I'm talking about homie. We out."

S-B looked at Ray-J and nodded as they put the murder one masks over their face. The party was still lit. Ray-J opened the SUV doors holding the M16 in his hand. He ran up to Tigger and yelled out, "Browns motherfuckers!"

Tigger turned around and just felt the bullets ripping through his body as his breath was being taken away from him. All you heard was people yelling and screaming as the gun blasts were going off. Tina went to turn around and run when S-B shot her three times in the chest, killing her. Rock looked at Tina's body on the ground when Ray-J yelled out to him. "Yo, nigga."

Rock turned around and looked at him as Ray-J shot him in the face, blowing it off with the M16.

Then, Ray-J turned around and shot the party up, shooting everyone he could see before running back to the SUV with SB as SB pulled off. You had Gangstar and a few other go-gettas running out to the streets, shooting at the truck as it pulled off. Gangstar looked around at all the dead bodies lying on the ground. It was a total of five. Showtime ran up to Gangstar.

"Yoo, Gangstar it was them Browns niggas. They yelled it out before they started shooting the block up."

"Showtime, Cash want war. It's time to burn the fucking city down."

Chapter 4

Big Apple walked up to Cash and dapped him up.

"Damn nigga, you got big as fuck. What the fuck was you doing, just working out and eating?"

"Shit ain't nothing else to do in that motherfucker and I ain't playing no fucking ball with dreams of being a NBA player. Nigga, I'm a thug, gangbanging with tattoos."

"Nigga I already know, but check this shit out. Last night shit went boom. Five of them niggas got toe tagged. You know how we rock. Gang gang, Browns nigga."

"Already but we don't need no heat coming down on us. We need the police to have a bigger problem on they hands than some gangbanging shit."

"You know what you are right, Big Apple. What you got in mind?"

"Let me take care of that. You just keep the shooters on the block, and I'll take care of everything else."

"Say less, my nigga. It's on and popping."

"I already fucking know. homie."

***

Gangstar sat in the barber seat, talking to a few of his homies when Detective Boatman walked into the barbershop. Everyone looked up at him but did not say a word. Gangstar stood up and walked up to Detective Boatman.

"What's up? You must need a cut or something, Detective. Maybe a lineup to get that new growth."

"No, I'm good on the cut, but I picked up a few of your guys last night. They got hit up pretty bad."

"I don't know none of them people who got killed but yeah, I heard about it. Shit sad as fuck, real talk."

"Yeah, it is. Just know that as long as these bodies keep dropping, it's going to be more than just me asking questions and coming around."

"Yeah, I know. Hopefully y'all can get to the bottom of this and stop all these innocent people from getting killed."

"You know what? At the end of the day, I hope you are still standing when the fire is out and the smoke is cleared out of the kitchen."

"That's the thing, Detective, I been in the kitchen when it was blazing hot flames everywhere and I was still standing. I never got burned."

"It's a new day and Big Apple is home. I think a lot of people are going to get burned. I'll see you around Gangstar."

"Yeah, you will Detective." Detective Boatman smiled as he walked out of the barber shop. Gangstar looked around at all of his guys and said, "Y'all see this shit?" Y'all see what the fuck is going on? I got the police at my fucking door. All because Tigger ain't take care of the fucking business like I told him to. Five fucking dead bodies! Yo Showtime, it's time that Cash hear that pop. Put the word out on the streets."

"Already, Gangstar." Gangstar ain't say nothing as he looked at Detective Boatman's car pulling off.

***

Detective Cross was looking around the burnt-down house and the three dead bodies inside, when Captain Moore walked up to him.

"What a fucking shit show we got here, Detective Cross? What can you tell me about this horrible massacre?"

"Three dead bodies. Father throat cut from ear to ear, mother shot in the head two times execution style, son shot to death as well. Then, they set the house on fire."

"What can you tell me about them?"

"Nothing, really. The father's name was Chad Wright, 42 years of age, worked in a warehouse for the last 16 years. Mother name was Lisa Wright, 39 years of age, school teacher for the last 7 years. Son name is Josh Wright, age 25. He worked at Dunkin Donuts. None of them had a criminal record. All of them were clean. This just don't make sense to me."

"Yeah, you make a good point. See what you can dig up and let me know. Let's see if we can make sense of all of this."

"I'm on it, Captain." Captain Moore looked around one more time before walking off.

Chapter 5

Cash walked into the kitchen, and looked at the females cooking up his dope, when Ray-J walked up to him. Cash smiled as he dapped him up.

"I heard you had the drum on the M16 last night."

"I let out like 300 rounds, clapping whatever I fucking saw, on Browns."

"I already know, bro. SB told me you wasn't playing at all."

"Man, you said get them. I said got it. I ain't do no talking really. I said what I said and rolled that nigga."

"What you say to him?"

"Browns motherfucker!"

"That's my fucking hitta. You stamped that shit. You tagged that shit. Browns never forget that. You are a baby OG now." Cash dapped Ray-J up before walking off.

***

"A lot of people go from brave to bitch when them bullets start to fly but Cash is different. He go from shooter to killer. It's like he's possessed with a demon. His wires ain't right. He built different. Some people just need to be dead or put in prison." Showtime was talking to Gangstar on 45th Street as they smoked they blunt.

"Real talk. Fuck that nigga. That nigga bleed like the rest of us. Showtime, this shit is going to be like taking candy from a baby. We going to kick this nigga door in and flatline that pussy. That nigga killed your cousin and both aunties and her son. I ain't letting that shit ride."

"Nigga I was just venting. We are going to peter roll that nigga and whoever is standing with him."

"Alright then, let's catch these bodies then, playboy."

"What time we riding out tonight?"

"10pm on the head."

"Say less then, homie. Let's eat our food tonight."

"Now, you got your head in the fucking game." Gangstar dapped Showtime up before walking to his car.

***

"B-God, they say life comes down to a series of moments and in those moments are choices, decisions that we make that could affect our lives forever. We are in one of the worst fights we have ever been in. All you need to think about and the one thing that needs to keep echoing in your mind is how we got here and how do we kill these motherfuckers."

B-God looked at Big Apple and nodded.

"Gangstar the nigga that's calling the shots. Showtime is just his do boy in so many words."

"So then, we cut the head off the snake and watch the body die. Last week was just the pre-show, it's time for the main event. Bang bang, homie."

"Let's pop the bottle then and show these motherfuckers how Browns roll."

"That's what the fuck I'm talking about. Let's ride out." Big Apple started up the BMW and drove off playing Cardi B When It's Up."

"B-God, remember you killed this nigga Showtime peoples in that drive by. Keep your eyes open because niggas want blood."

"Already."

Chapter 6

Gangstar walked to the front of the club, pass the line right to the doors where he was treated like a king. He was treated with the utmost respect. You had people that was standing in line watching him and Showtime walk past the metal detectors. Gangstar was dapping people up as he walked into the club as if he was a superstar. He walked all the way to the VIP seats, where the waiter brung him two bottles of Cîroc on a bucket of ice.

"Yo, this club is popping tonight. Super fucking lit, hands down, Gangstar," Showtime said as he was popping his shit, holding a bottle of Cîroc in his hand dancing to Lil-Baby's Pure Cocaine.

"This spot is most definitely popping tonight. This is what I need to clear my mind, real talk, bro." Gangstar was light skin with deep, dark waves, hazy eyes. He was 6 ft even with a deadly demeanor about him with a full beard and a slim build. Showtime was dark skin with long locks, tattoos on his face. He was a real killer. Five foot eight who feared nothing. On the other side of the club, Freestyle and Rip walked into the club to the VIP seats and sat down with two bad ass females.

"Yo Freestyle, Cash put the word out that it's on and popping with them and Gangstar on sight. And anyone yelling Go-Getters, see food, eat food or be food."

"You already know how I'm giving it up. I ain't doing no talking. Fuck that chit chat shit. Bang bang Browns Gang."

"That's what the fuck I'm talking about. Now let's enjoy our night. Pop those bottles and bring these bitches home with us."

"Real talk, we lit, Rip. Fuck it, Browns." Freestyle yelled out.

***

"Big Apple, now that you are home you see how shit is popping off. We running shit. Half this shit is yours, Browns is running shit."

Big Apple pulled his blunt and nodded before talking, "We can't say we own the streets till we put Gangstar and his crew down, homie."

"Word is already on the streets. Shoot on sight. Fuck Gangstar. Fuck Showtime. Niggas wanted smoke, now the kitchen on fire. See who can stand the fucking heat."

"Now that's what the fuck I like to hear. And don't even worry about the police. Detective Boatman and Detective Cross got they hands full I promise you that."

"Let's get to this bag then, Big Apple."

"Let's get to it."

***

"Yo bro, it's late as fuck. Two bottles of Cîroc got me leaning. I'm trying to bring these bitches with me, Gangstar."

"Nigga come on, let's get the fuck up out of here. I'm bent like a motherfucker too. I can't even stand up right."

Both of them started laughing as they was walking out front. Freestyle looked and saw Gangstar. He patted Rip on the shoulder and pointed at Gangstar. Rip looked at Gangstar and Showtime walking with the two females out of the club. He pulled his gun out and started shooting at them along the side of Freestyle. Bullets were flying everywhere. People were screaming and running everywhere. Showtime fell on the ground. Gangstar picked him up as blood splattered on his face from the impact of Freestyle's bullets. Gangstar watched as a lady's body hit the ground. He helped Showtime in the car, pulled his gun out and started shooting back at Rip and Freestyle. Bullets were flying everywhere. Rip and Freestyle ducked down so they wouldn't get hit. All you heard was car tires peeling off. Freestyle and Rip looked up and saw the white-on-white BMW peeling off and the few dead bodies on the ground.

Chapter 7

Cash sat in the room watching the news about the 4 dead people at the nightclub. They were talking about the shooting and how it took place. When B-God walked into the door, Cash looked at him and said, "4 dead bodies but none of them was any of the Go-Gettas. This is just more heat on the city for an empty cause."

"Look, Freestyle and Rip seen them boys and popped the bottle. No questions asked."

"Yeah, they did that, but now there's going to be more police on our ass than ever before."

"The police got more important shit on their plate than some gang shit. They worried about that crazy ass serial killer going around killing whole fucking families."

"Yeah, that is some sick ass shit. Now that's a motherfucker that needs to be locked up. Get word to Rip and Freestyle to come see me."

***

Gangstar looked at Symone as she walked into the trap house. Symone was 5-foot-5, dark skin, beautiful brown eyes with a banging, banging body. She had an hourglass shape. She was always down to ride for the set. Gangstar loved her loyalty. Symone walked into the trap up to Gangstar and gave him a hug and kiss on the cheek.

"How you feeling, papi, you alright?"

"Yeah, I'm 100, hands down. You know it's going to take more than two shooters to lay me the fuck down but real talk them niggas did have me down bad."

"Yeah, I heard. How is Showtime?"

"He's good but look, this is what I'm going to need from you. One of the little niggas that popped at me name is Freestyle. I need you to find that nigga and roll his ass."

"You know I got you."

"Good. Take care of that business. It's about to be a bloody summer."

"I got you. I think one of my homegirls knows where he lives but I'll let you know something this week." Symone walked up to Gangstar and kissed his cheek before walking away. Gangstar just watched as she walked off looking like a Barbie.

***

Big Apple had his eyes closed, licking his lips as he had this little baddie from the hood named Jazmine sucking his dick in his G-wagon. When his phone went off, he looked and saw Cash calling him. He looked at Jazmine and stopped her.

"Hold on, hold on, my mans is calling me." Big Apple picked the phone up and answered it, "Cash, what's the word?"

Cash pulled on his cigar before talking, "I know you heard about Rip and Freestyle letting off on Gangstar last night in the club."

"Yeah, I heard that shit went boom but niggas missed they target. That make shit look bad on us.""Yeah, that's what I was calling you about. How you want to deal with this now?"

"Ain't shit to deal with. Gangstar got the motherfucking message. Niggas know it's shoot on sight. All them niggas are plates. Them niggas sparked the fire that's about to burn they ass down."

"Say less, homie. Pull up on me later."

"Copy that." Big Apple hung the phone up and placed his hand back on Jazmine's head as she finished sucking his dick in the G-wagon. He leaned back and closed his eyes.

Chapter 8

Showtime picked up the phone and called Cash. After a few seconds, Cash picked up.

"Who the fuck is this?"

"Showtime, nigga!"

"You still breathing. You ain't dead yet, nigga."

"You talking real tough and you know you ain't about that fucking life. Your shooters missed, nigga."

"Don't worry. I got more coming straight at you, pussy. You know what time it is, nigga. We don't do the chat chit."

"I'm just letting you know that it's blood in the water, pussy. It's on and popping. Get ready to lay down."

Before Cash could say a word, Showtime hung up the phone and looked at Killer-B and Money.

"It's Showtime. Rutland Ave, Poppin Ave. Symone told me that's where they do most of they pickups and drop offs. Hit every fucking thing. I want it all!"

"We on that shit now, family and our bullets ain't going to miss. On Gang Gang."

"I already know, Money."

Showtime pulled his blunt as Money and Killer-B walked out of the spot to go stand on business.

***

Trap stepped out of the car with the duffle bag over his shoulder. He was walking up to the drop off, when Money ran up behind him and shot him 5 times in the back, killing him. He ran up to him grabbed the bag he had and ran back to the car where Killer-B was. They peeled off.

"Yeah, that's what the fuck I'm talking about, baby. One down and 10 kilos in this bag. Let's get this money!"

***

B-God paced the floor as he talked on the phone in a state of rage.

"You got to be fucking kidding me! Trap and who else got popped."

"Stone and Wild Style got rolled and all together it's 25 kilos that we got hit for."

"Fuck, okay, Rip. Let me call Cash and let him know what the fuck just happened."

"Copy that." Rip hung up the phone and called Cash. After a few rings, Cash picked up the phone.

"What's the vibe, Rip?"

'Shit is super ugly right now. We lost 3 runners and 25 birds. All those niggas got hit today."

"What the fuck you mean we lost 3 runners and 25 birds."

"Motherfuckers was waiting on them when they pulled up. They got they top popped and they bag got."

"You mean to tell me niggas is hitting my workers like we are fucking soft."

"Niggas is dropping like flies right now."

"Pull all the workers off the streets. I need to make some calls."

"Doing that now."

Cash hung up the phone and pulled his blunt, knowing Gangstar was a dead man walking. On Browns.

***

"That's what the fuck I'm talking about. Niggas want to play in these streets, then bodies are going to drop. My fucking shooters don't miss," Gangstar said as he was holding up a kilos of cocaine that Money and Killer-B brought him.

"We flipped 3 of them niggas. They ain't even see it coming. That shit was like taking candy from a baby."

"Y'all niggas just be on point cause these niggas are going to pop and when they do shit is going to get real ugly real fast. I know how Cash play. Gun, knives and bullets."

"Fuck that nigga. He pull up on this side of town and I'ma body that nigga, and that's on Go-Getters." Gangstar respected Money. He was a real killer. He was young and ain't give a fuck at all about laying the murder game down. He was a monster and niggas feared him.

Chapter 9

"Sometimes it's not about what you did, it's about what the people around you did, or some shit you did and another life. What they did with the black mask over their face looking down at the victims with tears in their eyes. Them being tied down to the chair and their dead dog laying in a pool of blood. Each victim had the sharp knife blade to their throats and one by one their throat was cut. They slit them wide open as rivers of blood came pouring out. Just watching the blood pour out of their throats was a rush to see. They walked to the living room wall and wrote in blood 7. Then, they took the bloody knife and stabbed it into the wall with the bloody duct tape hanging from it. They walked over to the dog and poured gas all over him. They were out of the front door as they lit a single match, dropping it and watching the house go up in flames as they made they way off the block without being seen.

***

Detective Cross looked around the crime scene, in disbelief at what he was seeing. More dead bodies. More innocent lives that were taken. He walked over to the wall where there was the number 7 painted in blood on the walls with a roll of bloody duct tape. That's when Detective Boatman walked up behind him.

"This is fucking crazy."

Detective Cross turned around and looked at him. "Who the fuck you telling? This is the sixth killing within the last two months. We have us a sick puppy on our hands."

"Who called it in?"

"A neighbor. She saw the flames in the house and called 911."

Detective Boatman looked outside the front window and saw the many people standing around. "Cross, this don't look good at all. We have a fucking gang war going on right now and a psychopath running around killing people."

"Yeah, I know this is a shit storm that's about to come our way."

"What do we know about our victims?"

"All I know right now is that it was a family of three. Mother, her two sons and dog."

"Yeah, it's going to be a long night. Need me to stick around?"

"Yeah, that will be good, Boatman."

***

You had 20 plus police officers on the scene, yellow police tape blocking the crime scene off. You heard the cries of the family member and friend of the victims. The flashing red and blue lights reflection showed off the wet pavement outside the victims' house. Gangstar and Showtime walked up to the crime scene and looked around. Ki Ki walked up to Gangstar and hugged him as she cried in his arms.

"Ki Ki. What happened out here tonight?" With tears in her eyes and broken words she said, "Someone killed them, tied them up and killed them brutally. Then, they left the knives in my auntie's head, cut my little cousin's throat wide open, and set the dog on fire. The next-door neighbor saw the flames and called the police, but they got here too late. They all was dead already, Gangstar."

"Damn, Ki Ki. I'm sorry to hear that, fuck. That's crazy, hands down."

Showtime just watched as they brought all three of the dead bodies out of the house in black bags. He looked at Gangstar as he was hugging Ki Ki as she cried on his shoulders.

***

Freestyle sat on the hood of his car, smoking a blunt when he saw Symone walking his way. She was looking so sexy with her dark chocolate skin sucking on a lollipop.

"What's up, Style."

"It's crazy. I don't even know your sexy ass, but you know my name. Did we meet before or something?"

"No, Candy told me who you was. I was asking about you."

Style looked over at Candy on the stairs talking to a few of her homegirls. Style just smiled at her

"So, what's your name, beautiful?"

"Symone with a Y not a I."

"That's cute. Where you from? I ain't never see you on this side of town before."

"I'm from Brooklyn, but enough about me. I'm trying to get to know you."

"Is that so?"

"Yeah, it is."

"I like your style. You straight forward. How about we get the fuck up out of here?"

"That sounds like a plan to me."

Style jumped off the hood of his car and opened the door for Symone to get inside. He then walked around the car and looked at Candy one more time as he winked at her before getting in driving off.

"So, what you trying to do? Get something to eat, chill, what's up?"

"It don't matter. I'm riding out with you. Whatever you want to do."

"Say that then." Style blasted the music as he drove off with Symone.

***

Cash pulled up to the warehouse and stepped out of his Hummer along with Big Apple. He walked inside and looked around at everyone with an expression on his face. He was pissed off to the max.

"What I don't understand is how these motherfuckers knew where our drop offs was at. 25 kilos and three bodies. Somebody better start talking real fast because I want fucking answers now."

B-God walked up. "Niggas must have been watching us. We just ain't know. This shit right here fucked us all up."

Big Apple was looking at everyone. "Look, I think I know where Showtime baby mother stay at."

"Good, find out for sure. I need that address. The gloves are off. We are playing hard ball now. If y'all see a Go-Getta, y'all body a Go-Getta and anybody. Niggas, bitches and children. If they are wearing their colors, they are going to die with blood on them. One more thing, there's no more runs alone. 3 to a drop now."

Nobody said anything after Cash said that. They all just watched as he made his way back into the Hummer with Big Apple.

***

"Damn shorty I ain't know your head game was like this. You are the truth, hands down," Freestyle said as Symone was sucking and licking all over his dick. He grabbed her head and started fucking her face as she was taking all his dick in her throat. He grabbed her head as he nutted all down

33

her throat. He pulled his dick out and looked a Symone as she was licking the nut off her lips.

"Damn sexy, you are the truth. What the fuck."

"I'm glad you like. There's more where that came from."

"So, won't you pull your pants down so I can lick that pussy and beat the kitty up for you, baby girl."

"No. I sucked your dick, daddy. That was to let you know what type of bitch I am, but my mouth is dry. Can you get me something to drink?"

"Yeah, I got you, baby girl. I'll be right back." Freestyle pulled up his pants and walked out the room, leaving Symone on the bed.

Once Freestyle was gone, Symone pulled her phone out and texted Gangstar.

The text said 2152 Hillside Dr. He's here by himself.

Gangstar replied back. Sending Killa-B and Money to you now.

Symone replied back. *Kopy.*

She then placed her phone down on the bed as Freestyle was walking back into the room. She got up and walked over to him. Taking the glass out of his hand, taking a sip of the soda. He looked to see her phone vibrating. Symone looked at him and rushed to her phone. That's when Freestyle pulled his gun out and pointed it at her face.

"Bitch give me your phone before I blow your shit off now."

Freestyle walked over to Symone and took her phone. He read the text message from Gangstar, and smacked her in the face, knocking her out cold. Then, he called Cash up as he looked at her laying on the floor.

Chapter 10

Symone opened her eyes in the basement, tied down to a chair. She heard voices but couldn't see anything because there was a bag over her head.

"So, this bitch right here tried to set you up?"

"Shit was crazy. She just got done sucking my dick and all I went to get her a glass of juice and she done text this nigga Gangstar. She gave him my addy and all so you know I smacked her in the face with the Hummer and knocked her out. I called you and here I am now."

Cash looked at her, then walked over to Symone and pulled the bag off her head. He looked down at her. "You know you done fucked up, right?" Symone just looked up at Cash as Big Apple walked over to them.

"So, what you want to do with this bitch?"

"Let's see how much she worth to Gangstar. Get that bitch phone and call him up. Let's talk numbers."

Big Apple took Symone phone and called up Gangstar. After a few rings, he picked up.

"Yo, where you at? Money and Killa-B went to the house. No one was there." Big Apple looked at Cash and shook his head

"I got your bitch. She was sloppy with the texts and fumbled the ball, nigga. She is really a baddie but the bitch is tied down right now. She can't talk."

"Who the fuck is this?"

"Big Apple, pussy. Now let's talk numbers. You got me for 25 kilos and 3 bodies. I'm asking for 50 kilos back now or I'm send this bitch body back chopped up. Test my Gangstar, now."

Gangstar looked at Showtime. Showtime shook his head, then through his hand up and said in a relaxed voice, "Fuck that bitch." As he looked at Gangstar.

"Y'all niggas could suck my dick. That bitch could suck my dick. I'll see y'all niggas in the streets."

Gangstar hung up the phone after saying that. Symone looked at Cash with tears in her eyes not because she was scared but the disloyalty Gangstar just showed.

"It looks like you was loyal to a nigga who ain't give a fuck about you, lil mama." Big Apple walked over to Symone and place the shotgun to her head. Symone ain't blink or nothing.

"You ready to hear that pop, bitch?"

Symone closed her eyes and ain't say nothing. Cash respected that. He placed his hand on top of the gun and lowered it as he looked at Symone.

"You ain't going to die today. Me and you are going to have a talk. Untie her and put her in my car. We are going back to my place."

Big Apple looked at Cash crazy as hell but he respected his call.

***

Detective Boatman and Detective Cross sat in Captain Moore's office not saying nothing as Captain Moore looked over the pictures of the victims of the serial killer. Captain Moore rubbed his head before talking, "Detectives, what do y'all have for me? 6 victims to this serial killer. These killings been all over the news, day and night. What can y'all tell me?"

"Sir, we don't have no leads at all. All we know is that the killer likes to use a knife in all his killings. He picks the victims of family homes," Detective Cross said.

"I don't want y'all working on no other case until we find this sick son of a bitch. Do I make myself clear?"

"As water, sir."

"Good. Both of y'all can go."

Both detectives got up and walked out of the office.

Detective Cross looked at Boatman "There's more to this case than we are seeing. I just can't put my fucking finger on it right now."

"Let's hit the streets and see what the fuck we can find out then."

"And what about these two gang wars going on right now?"

"Fuck them. We will deal with that later. Right now, let's see what we can figure out about that serial killer."

"After you, you are the lead Detective."

"You ain't shit, Cross."

They both started laughing.

Chapter 11

"Help me help you now. I just saved your life after you tried to get one of my men killed." Cash lit his cigar while looking at Symone at the table. She was quiet. She ain't say nothing as he talked.

"So, you didn't kill me because you want me to be a rat?"

"No, I want you to join a winning and loyal team. I respect that you ain't beg for your life and you ain't cry. That's why I kept you alive. That was some real G shit, hands down."

"I been in the streets all my life. I'm numb to pain. I just thought that Gangstar was going to be more loyal to me than what I heard. I was a fool for thinking that."

"Look, them doors is opened anytime you want to leave, but if you want a loyal family that's going to back you one hundred percent, I got you right here with me and mine. We don't leave our homie to the wolves."

"So, what I have to do to be a part of this family?"

"You know what Browns stand for?"

"No I don't."

"Believe Real Ones Will Never Snitch. You had a chance to tell and you ain't. I respect that. After Gangstar shitted on you, you kept it one hundred. That's all I needed to see."

Symone thought for a second, not saying a word.

"Promise me you will protect me, and y'all will hold me down."

"You got my word. On the set, but if you fuck over me and mines, I'll kill you in the worst fucking way. On gang."

"I won't. You have my word."

"Good. You can drive me around now."

Symone followed Cash outside to Cash's black on black G-wagon. He threw her the keys as he got into the backseat.

"Where we headed?"

"To the warehouse. It's time for you to meet the family."

"And where's that at?"

"Poppin Ave."

Symone pulled off as Cash rode in the backseat, smoking his cigar. He knew he was taking a gamble with her but in his heart testing her loyalty was worth the risk.

***

"So, what now homie?" Gangstar asked Showtime.

"We get ready to eat our food, because 9 out of 10 times, Symone is dead. Cash wants smoke, so let's burn the fucking city down because bullets is loading up and about to fly."

"Fuck it. Shoot or get shot. Let the guns blaze now."

Gangstar pulled his blunt with his mind made up. It's war. He looked at Showtime while cleaning both his guns.

***

B-God opened the warehouse doors when he saw Cash's G-wagon pulling up. All eyes was on Symone as she stepped out of the truck. Cash doors opened and the first thing he said was, "SB, Freestyle, Rip, B-God, Ray-J come here."

Once everyone was standing next to him he said, "Symone is a part of this family now. Y'all will treat her and respect her as part of this family and this is the only time I'm going to say this. Freestyle, you and Symone go have a personal conversation."

Symone walked off with Freestyle as B-God walked up to Cash.

"You think it was smart to put her down?"

"She was just loyal to a man she heard say fuck that bitch. She ain't rat on his ass or beg for her life. Yeah, it was the right move to make. Plus, I need a driver. When she get done talking with Freestyle, show her some love. Give her like 3 Gs in front of the family and a half of bird. She's the key to Gangstar's downfall."

"Say less, you are the boss."

Cash looked at Symone talking to Freestyle in the corner.

"Look, it wasn't personal. I was just doing what I had to do for the set. That's all." Symone reasoned.

"Not long ago, you tried to roll me. How can I trust you because you stayed a few nights with Cash? Now you are Browns?"

"Look you have all rights not to like me, you do but I'm here now and you have my word that I got your back."

"So, did Candy know you were down with the Go-Gettas?"

"No she ain't. I knew her from school. That's all."

"We will see where your loyalty stands because if you fuck my family over, I will be the first to put a bullet in your head and that's on Browns."

"Well, I don't have to worry about that then."

Freestyle looked at Symone one more time and walked off as B-God walked up to her. She had water in her eyes as he handed her 3Gs in 100-dollar bills.

"That's some love from the family and this is to keep you afloat."

"Thank y'all," Symone said as he gave her the half of bird.

"No sweat homie, you Browns now."

"For life."

Cash waved Symone over as he smoked his cigar while getting back in the G-wagon. He was letting her know it was time to go.

Chapter 12

"Yo Money, am I tripping?" Killer-B asked him as he walked over to Money looking at the hot dog truck.

"What you talking about?"

"Look over there next to that hot dog truck. Is that Symone wearing all brown with a brown flag around her neck?"

"Dead ass. That's her. Come on, let's pull up on that bitch."

Symone watched as they was walking to her through the glass on the hot dog truck. She pulled her Glock-40 out and waited for them to be right behind her to point it at them.

"Symone, what the fuck you got going on wearing those colors?" Money asked her.

Symone turned around holding her gun in her hand, looking at Money and Killer-B.

"Y'all see what the fuck it is. Y'all niggas left me for dead so fuck y'all niggas. Fuck Gangstar and Showtime. Browns, pussies."

Killer-B went to swing on Symone when she said that with no hesitation. Symone shot Killer-B two times in the chest and took off running. Money pulled his gun out, shooting at her. Money looked down at Killer-B as blood was coming out his mouth. He was taking his last breath. Money looked around and took off running, leaving Killer-B's dead body lying in a pool of blood. Symone got down on him and was ready to do it again if she had to. Browns was her family now and she just stamped that.

***

Gangstar looked at Showtime as he walked up to him smoking a blunt.

"Yo, Money just called."

"Word, and what Money talking about?"

"He said Symone just killed Killer-B and she flying Browns colors now."

Gangstar stood up, looking crazy. "That bitch is yelling Browns, and she just bodied Killer. Yeah, she just lost her fucking mind. Put a bird on that bitch head!"

"Already done."

"Where is Money at now?"

"Laying low. They had a shootout on Main Street. When shit cool down he will be coming this way."

"Make sure you bring him to see me ASAP."

"Kopy that."

Gangstar pulled his phone out and called Symone. After a few rings, she picked up.

"You must have a fucking death wish. You know you are a dead bitch, right."

"No nigga, fuck what you are talking about. Suck my dick, I'll see you in the streets, pussy." Symone hung up the phone, knowing the bridge she had just burned down. She was ready for whatever came her way. Her bullets flew just like theirs, she said to herself.

***

"Big Apple, shit just went boom."

Big Apple looked at Ray-J "What the fuck you talking about shit just went boom?"

"Some of them Go-Gettas just ran down on Symone and she bodied one of them. It was a crazy shootout, but she got up out of there."

"When this shit pop off and where?"

"This shit just went down about an hour ago on Main Street."

"Where she at now?"

"The warehouse."

"Did you call Cash?"

"No, I called you first."

"I'm going to go check the scene out. You call Cash and let him know what just popped off."

"Okay, I'll do that now and go to the warehouse with Symone to one of us get there."

"Copy that."

Big Apple hung up the phone, picked his gun up off the table, grabbed his car keys and walked out of the front door. Cash was right. He said to himself. Symone was ready. She just needed the right team behind her.

***

Showtime was on Main Street looking at the scene as the police was taking pictures of Killer-B's body laid out in front of the hot dog truck. Big Apple pulled up on the scene looking around. He stepped out of his car and watched as close as he could to the yellow caution tape where Killer-B'ds dead body was. He looked and him and Showtime caught eye contact. It was a stare that would have put the fear in death's eyes Big Apple pointed at Showtime with his hands as if he had a gun in his hand and fired a shot at him. Showtime stuck up his middle finger at him and turned around and walked off. Detective Boatman and Detective Cross seen that from both of them as they both walked off

"There you have it, Detective Boatman. One coming to see his dead homie and the other one looking to make sure the job is done. Now we know the faces behind the gang war."

"You're right. Now, let's do a background check on them both."

"Copy that."

Chapter 13

Cash walked up to Symone as she was sitting down, smoking a blunt. She was holding her gun in her hand with her head down.

"You good?"

"Yeah, I'm straight."

"What happened out there today?"

"Killer-B and Money pulled up on me talking crazy, so I smoked Killer-B ass and shot it out with Money."

"You put that work in. I'm proud of you."

That's when both of them looked at the door and saw Big Apple walking in and right up to them.

"What's the word, Apple?"

"I just left Main Street. That shit is ugly up there right now. She left that nigga dead with his eyes open."

"Well, you know what they say. When you die with your eyes open, you deserved that shit. Homie looking up at the stars."

"Yeah, that bitch is flooded with police right now."

"Good, now niggas know we ain't playing. Ray-J, you and SB go do a drive by on Gangstar spot. Symone, go show them where it's at."

Symone nodded.

"Cash I got some shit to do tonight. I'll pull up on y'all in a little while, bro."

"Kopy that." Big Apple dapped everyone up before walking off back to his car.

45

"Y'all niggas ride out tonight at 9 and make sure that shit is bloody."

"Say less, Cash," Ray-J said holding his gun in his hand.

***

B-God walked to his car and went to open the door. That's when he seen Gangstar walking up on him with his gun in his hand. He turned his head and seen Money standing there. B-God punched Money in the face then turned around and went to swing on Gangstar. Gangstar shot him two times in the chest, dropping him. B-God was trying to catch his breath, coughing up blood when Money stood over top of him. He pointed his gun at B-God face and shot him two times, killing him. Gangstar patted Money on the back and kicked B-God's dead body.

"Come on. We got to get the fuck from over here now."

"Pussy nigga."

Both of them ran to Gangstar's car and pulled off, leaving B-God dead in a pool of blood in front of the project building. They had been watching him, waiting on him to leave out. They caught their body, leaving B-God with blood in his mouth and tears in his eyes. They were letting it be known opps cry before they die.

***

Rip called Cash. After a few seconds, Cash picked up.

"What's the vibe bro?"

"I'm over here in the 40s. They caught B-God down bad. He's dead, bro. Shot all up in the face. Shit is fucked up."

"Bro, you have to be fucking kidding me."

"Wish I was bro. The homie flatlined."

"Find out who he was going to see and hit me back."

"Copy that."

SB hung up the phone and just looked around, lost for words. Even the thuggest nigga had tears in their eyes for they dead homie. SB wiped the tears out his eyes and walked off.

Chapter 14

"What the fuck happened out there last night, Gangstar?"

Gangstar pulled his blunt before talking, "An eye for an eye, my nigga. I got a call last night about B-God and we went and rolled his ass. No talking, just gangbanging. The Go-Getta way."

"That's what the fuck I'm talking about, homie."

"Make sure everyone is on point because they are going to hit back, and we don't know what Symone told them."

"I already know how that bitch get down. We should have been offed her ass but say less. I'm getting on that shit now."

"Good. Keep me posted on everything."

"Will do."

Gangstar watched as Showtime walked out of the room to handle the business.

***

"Symone, I need to know where Showtime or Gangstar stay at. It's time we hit them hard, you feel me?"

"On Browns, I don't know where they stay. All I know is that Showtime's baby mom live off of Avon. That's it."

"Say less homie, that's good enough." Cash looked at SB and Rip and nodded letting them know to go get that bitch. Symone knew what she did was fucked up, but within the last few weeks, Cash showed her more loyalty than Gangstar ever did. He made sure she had a new spot and all to lay her head at and he was making sure she was eating.

***

Cash sat quietly in the backseat of the BMW, smoking a cigar and looking at Showtime's baby mother's house.

"Symone, are you sure that's the house?"

"Yeah, that's her house. I been there before."

"Good, let's take care of the business then." Cash pulled out his phone and called Ray-J. After a few seconds, Ray-J picked up.

"Yeah, boss."

"Bring her and the two kids out. Then, set the place on fire. If there's anybody else in the house, kill them but I want his kids and baby moms brought back to me alive."

"Copy that."

Ray-J hung up the phone and looked at Freestyle and Rip as he put the murder 1 mask over his face. "He said burn the house down and kill everyone but the girl and his kids."

"Fuck it, let's do this then," Rip said.

Cash watched as they ran up in the house. All you heard was gunshots rang off and all you saw the flash from the gun being shot.

"Bitch shut the fuck up.! You know what the fuck this is. Thank your bitch ass baby daddy, bitch. Now, come on before I put one of these bullets in your fucking head, hoe," Ray-J said as he dragged her out the house at gun point. Rip carried the two children to the van. Freestyle looked around the house at the two dead bodies. He then heard a voice in the closet. He opened the door and saw an old lady there with tears in her eyes, looking at him.

"I don't know what my son did, but his children are innocent of his crimes. Don't punish the children for their father's deeds."

"Let me tell you this old lady, when the devil knocks on the door, he don't give a fuck who he punish to get his point across." Rip looked at Ray-J.

"Yo, go see what's taking him so long. We got to get the fuck up out of here before them boys in blue come."

"Say less." Ray-J ran into the house and looked at Freestyle pointing the gun at Showtime's mother's head.

"Yo, who the fuck is this bitch? Where she come from?"

"Showtime's mother."

Ray-J smiled. He grabbed her by the arm and brought her to the van. A few seconds later, the house went up in flames full force.

"Oh shit."

Cash looked at Symone when she said that. "Who is that bitch they are bringing to the van?"

"Showtime's mother."

"And they say you can't have your cake and eat it too. Driver let's go, now."

Cash smiled. The ball was in his court now and he had no limitation on the shit he would do to get his point across.

***

"Showtime, shit just got ugly," Gangstar said as he walked up to him, shaking his head.

"What the fuck are you talking about?"

"Money just called me. He said you baby ma's house is in flames and the police just pulled two dead bodies out of there."

Showtime couldn't believe what he was hearing. He pulled his phone out and called her but she ain't pick up. He looked at Gangstar.

"What the fuck you mean?"

Showtime took off running out of the house to his car. He took off, headed to his baby mother's house. It took him 20 minutes to get there. The road was blocked off by all the police cars and fire trucks. He stepped out of the car and walked up to see the house still in full flames as they was still fighting the fire to put it out. Showtime ran up to one of the officers.

"Sir, are there people still in the house?"

"No there's not. Do you know them?"

"Yes. This is my baby mother's house. Her name is Kisha."

The officers waved over Detective Boatman to him.

"Detective, this is his baby mother's house her name is Kisha."

Detective Boatman looked at Showtime and said, "I know you. I saw you the other day on Main Street. You and another guy had eye contact, and he made a gun up out of his hand and shot at you. You threw the bird up at him. What the fuck you got yourself mixed up in that it caused this house fire. Two dead bodies and four people to be kidnapped out of this house?"

Showtime looked around when Detective Boatman said that.

That's when he noticed his mother's car out front of the house. He closed his eyes and shook his head as tears filled his eyes.

"I don't know what you are talking about."

"Hey, officers."

"Yes, Detective?"

"Bring him to the precinct. He need to answer some questions for me."

"I don't know shit."

"Well, I'll be the judge of that." Detective Boatman looked around one more time before headed back to Detective Cross.

"Hey, I got the baby father in the car. I'm bringing him to the station to answer some questions."

"Copy that. I'll be down there once this all clears up and we put this fire out."

"Cool, I'll see you there," Detective Boatman said before walking off.

Chapter 15

"You want to talk? Or want to get that phone call that your mother is dead?" Showtime looked at Detective Boatman, not saying a word, knowing the laws of the street

"Okay, I'll talk first. The two dead people at the house were shot execution style in the back of the head. Y'all Go-Gettas have heart, but them Browns motherfuckers are ruthless, hardcore and no heart. You just remember that. Now I can help you if you give me something to work with."

"Look, I don't know what the fuck you are talking about. I don't know them dead motherfuckers. Now, if you ain't locking me up for something, you are holding me against my fucking will." Detective Boatman knocked two times on the desk. "You know what? You can go. I'll see you soon when you come to ID the bodies."

"Detective Boatman, right?"

"Yeah, that's me."

"Okay, suck my dick," Showtime said as he got up and walked out the investigation room.

Once outside, he pulled his phone out and called Gangstar. After a few rings, Gangstar picked up.

"Yo, I just got out of booking. They bagged me for checking on my baby moms. Bro, shit is super ugly right now."

"Bro ugly is an understatement. Niggas sent pictures to my phone of your moms and baby moms ass naked with their hands tied behind they back. They had a gun to they head, bro."

Showtime closed his eyes and bit down on his teeth as he yelled *FUCK* out loud. "Bro, did they say anything about my kids?"

"No, bro."

"Yo, I'm on the way to come get you now, family."

"Cool, I'm walking down Main Street, bro."

"Copy that."

Showtime had murder on his mind; he was ready to do anything to get back at Cash and bring his family back alive.

***

Big Apple sat in his car, smoking a blunt outside of the police station. He was across the street watching Detective Cross's car, waiting for him to come out of the police station. He waited patiently, knowing he was about to set the city on fire tonight. He had to let it be known what happens when you fuck with Browns business. Not even a badge could keep you safe in New York. Anybody could get it. Police too.

***

Showtime paced the floor waiting for his phone to ring with Gangstar and Money in the room.

"Showtime chill, keep calm. Niggas is going to call."

"How the fuck you sound, Gangstar? My people ass naked with gun to they fucking dome. You talking about calm down. Motherfuckers are going to die behind this one."

That's when the phone started to ring. Showtime picked the phone up.

"You must have a death wish."

"You talking real tough to a nigga that don't have shit in his control right now. Keep talking shit and I'll be your stepdaddy before the night is up."

"Man, what the fuck you want?"

"I'm thinking 60 kilos, $600,000. How does that sound?"

"Bro, I don't have that much right now."

"Call this number back in ten minutes and tell me what the fuck you got then."

Cash hung up the phone as he puffed on his cigar, waiting on Showtime to call him back.

He was thinking about sending him his mother's finger, but he knew he was going to kill her anyway.

***

Detective Cross came walking out of the police station with his briefcase in his hand. He was smoking a cigarette while headed to his car. Big Apple watched him as he got inside and backed up out of his parking space, headed down 110. Big Apple pulled his gun out and cocked it back. Detective Cross looked at Big Apple the other day on Main Street along with Detective Boatman. In Big Apple's eyes, there wasn't nothing worse than a witness, police or not.

Detective Boatman stopped at the red light. Big Apple pulled up beside his car and lowered his head as if he was about to light a cigarette. When Detective Cross turned his head, Big Apple pointed the gun at his head and started shooting at him. Detective Cross pressed the gas, taking off out of control and hitting a car coming across the intersection. Big Apple pulled up and jumped out the car, shooting Detective Cross multiple times in the chest and back.

As he was slumped over in the car, Big Apple ran back to his car and peeled off. The car that Detective Cross hit, the lady opened the car door, falling out. She got to her feet and called 911 from her phone. She looked at Detective Cross still in the car with blood coming out of his mouth. From the impact of the car crash, she couldn't tell if he was breathing or not.

***

Cash looked at his phone as it was ringing. He picked it up with a smile on his face.

"What's the fucking numbers?"

"I have 50 kilos 300,000. That's all I have bro. On God, man."

"I'll take that but that shit still going to cost you nigga. 2415 Lincoln Ave. Warehouse in the back. Drop everything off there. You have 20 minutes." Cash hung up the phone after saying that.

Showtime jumped in his car along with Money and Gangstar to make the drop off. It took him 10 minutes to get there. He stepped out of the car with Money and Gangstar, holding M16s as he placed the money and drugs where Cash told him to. He called him, letting him know the drop is done as they pulled off.

***

Detective Boatman rushed into the hospital to the 3rd floor where Detective Cross was in surgery. Captain Moore walked up to Detective Boatman.

"What happened to him, is he going to make it?"

"Yeah, Detective, he's going to make it. It was a close call. The son of a bitch had his vest on still under his jacket. He only got shot in the arm and leg. The vest protected his chest and back but someone wanted him dead. The impact of the car made him cough up blood but other than that the doctor said he should be fine."

"Good, what about the lady. Did she see anything?"

"All she said was she saw a man shooting then pulling off."

Detective Boatman walked off.

"Where you headed?"

"To go question her again." Without saying another word, Detective Boatman walked off.

***

Rip dropped the bag off on the table in front of Cash as cash smoked his cigar.

"50 kilos and $300,000 in cash."

"Good. It's time to take care of the business then." Cash got up, holding his gun as he walked to Showtime's mother, baby mother and children. He looked down at them and said,

"Your son and baby daddy crossed the line. He think shit is sweet with us. Some lines you just can't cross. With that being said, come on. It's time for me to drop y'all off." Cash opened the van door at the same drop off spot he had them tie his family up.

When Showtime's mother turned around, Cash had the gun pointed at her face. He pulled the trigger, blowing her brains out. Blood splattered all over Showtime's children and their mother. He then looked down at her as she was crying next to the kids and the kids was crying calling their mommy name.

"Next time it will be your fucking blood. Let Showtime know that shit and if I hear any word about this from the police, I'll come for your family. Cash looked at her, got in the van and pulled off before calling Showtime, letting him know where to find his family.

Chapter 16

Big Apple walked up on Cash as he was watching the females break down the kilos of cocaine as he was smoking his blunt.

"I see shit played out good for you last night. What you get out that boy?"

"50 kilos of cocaine, 300,000 in cash and a body. Really, three bodies."

"What you mean really three bodies?"

"Two niggas that was in the house. Plus that boy Showtime's moms. I personally left her breathless. Where the fuck was you at last night?"

"Pussy ass Detective saw me the other day down on Main Street threaten Showtime. So, you know I waited on that baby to put him down. I emptied the clip on his ass last night. I caught his ass at the red light and fired his ass up, bro."

"Real talk. I saw that shit on the news. You know that boy lived, right?"

The expression on Big Apple's face when Cash told him that was one of total disbelief. "Ain't no way in hell. That nigga must have had an angel over his ass. I ran up on that shit and fired all in the window."

"Nigga you must of had a 22 because son breathing. What I tell you about walking around with them pea-shooters."

"Fuck you, Cash," Big Apple said laughing as he walked away, not knowing how the fuck Detective Cross was still alive after taking all them shots. *Ain't no way in hell,* he said to himself.

***

Showtime sat on the steps with his gun in his hands, holding it with his face on the neck of the gun. Tears came out of his eyes, thinking about his mother laying on the wet grass with a bullet hole in the back of her head. All because of the life he lived. He was thinking about the many times she told him the life you live will cause you more than just pain but it will hurt your loved ones around you. Now, his mother is dead, his baby mother moved down south with his kids and he don't have nothing to show for it at all but blood and pain. He looked up when Money walked up on him.

"Ain't shit I can say to you right now that you want to hear. Just know when you are ready I'm ready to go with you to body those niggas, homie."

"Yo, that's love real talk. Good looking, Money."

"Always bro, hands down."

"Yo, take me to go see this nigga Gangstar. It's time we show those Browns niggas who the fuck we are."

"That's what the fuck I'm talking about. Let's ride out."

Chapter 17

Detective Cross opened his eyes to see Detective Boatman sleeping in the chair across from him in the hospital room. He was able to speak but only in a low tone.

"Boatman, Boatman."

Detective Boatman opened his eyes and looked at Detective Cross. "Look who decided to finally wake up after two days of sleep. How you feel?"

"I feel like I been hit by a fucking Mack truck."

"That means you are alive. Let me go get the nurse."

Detective Boatman walked out the room to get the nurse. A few seconds later, the nurse and doctor walked into the room side by side up to Detective Cross.

"How are you feeling, Detective Cross? You had me scared for a little while, but you made it through."

"How long is my body going to be sore like this for?"

"For the next few weeks. You are lucky to be alive. If you didn't have that vest on you will be dead. Six shots, hollow tip to the chest and six to the back. That vest you had on saved your life."

"How long do I have to be here before I can get back to work?"

"Within the next two weeks."

"Okay Doctor, thanks.

"No problem. Take it easy, Detective. You will be at one hundred percent in no time."

"Can't wait."

The doctor nodded his head as he walked out of the room with Nurse Joy.

***

"Come in and have a seat, Detective Boatman," Captain Moore said as she sat behind her desk with a thick case file in front of her.

"What can I do for you Captain?"

"I need answers, Detective. We have too many cases that's unsolved. Seven murders by a serial killer. Gang killings and one of our own was just shot twelve times. Are we losing our grip on NYC here?"

"With all due respect Captain, me and Detective Cross worked our ass off on this serial killer case. It's like they are doing it for sport. They're not taking anything. They are just killing people."

"Detective, do what you have to do to close one of those cases. I don't care what you have to do, just do it, okay?"

"Yes ma'am." Detective Boatman got up and walked out of the Captain's office, headed to his car. He now knew he can play by his own rules and say fuck the rule book.

Chapter 18

"Cash, you know I don't have a problem fucking with you, but you are hot right now. Every time I turn on the news I see murder, gang wars, this crazy ass serial killer and now a police shooting. You hot right now and I don't know if I want to fuck with that."

"Because I'm hot, you scared, Carlos. That's what you saying?"

"Nigga don't ever bring scary business to my fucking table. I killed more people in the worst way than you could ever imagine. Like I said, you hot and I know your name is attached to all this shit. I been seeing on the news, well maybe not the serial killing shit but everything else I can stamp that you have your name on it."

"Look, I'm just trying to get this money and this paper out the street. You are the king of your cartels, so let me ask you this. Name one king who ain't catch a few bodies on the way to his throne?"

Carlos thought about what Cash just said and smiled. "You and your fucking word play, Cash. 15 fucking years and you still ain't change. 20 kilos at 30,000 a pop. You get 40 and I'll drop the price down to 23,000 a pop. What do you want to do?"

"I want 50 kilos of that ninety-nine percent pure shit."

"Motherfucker all my shit is pure, and you know this shit. Look, Tuesday at 9:30 pm. Dock 27. Be there with the money, All big bills."

"Say less. I'll see you there." Cash dapped Carlos up before walking out of his penthouse. Carlos just looked at him as he lit his cigar, knowing Cash was hot but loyal to the end. He will see a grave before he sees prison walls again.

***

Showtime came walking out of the deli eating a bag of chips when Detective Boatman walked up to him, smoking a cigarette.

"I'm sorry about your loss. You and your family have my deepest condolences."

Showtime just looked at him.

"You really mean that shit? Or is that just something you wanted to say."

"No I really mean that. No child should have to go through that but I told you two weeks ago how this was going to play out."

"Bro, you don't know how shit really plays out in these streets. We play for two different teams. Remember that."

"You right. We do play for two different teams, but I know Gangstar ain't strike back yet. Ain't no way in hell shit like this is supposed to ride. Me and you both know Cash and his Browns crew is behind all of this shit, maybe even my partner's shooting. Look, fuck the law and fuck the code of the streets. Let's both break the rules and give those motherfuckers what they got coming to them." Detective Boatman puffed on his cigarette

"Yeah, and what's that?"

"A cold grave and a hot bullet. Get the nigga that killed your mother and let me put Cash in a 8 by 9 for the rest of his fucking life because I know he's the one that made the call on my partner's shooting."

"Understand if I do this, we ain't buddies, we ain't partner's and we damn sure ain't friends. This is just payback knocking at the devil's door and when this shit is over, you go your way and I'll go mine."

"That sounds good to me."

"Cool. I'll be in touch."

Showtime walked off, knowing this wasn't no police shit. This was personal and if he had to go against the street code so fucking be it. His mother wasn't going to die alone and sometimes you got to do what the fuck you got to do. Period.

Chapter 19

"So, let me get this right, Cash. I'm trying to make sense of all of this. We just got 50 kilos from Gangstar and his crew and you just ordered 50 more kilos from Carlos? What was the point of all that?"

"Apple think outside the box. 23,000 a brick. We can make 2 out of one. That's 100 kilos at 40,000 a pop, plus the 50 we got from Gangstar. The city is ours. Plus, we still needed the plug. How long do you think 50 birds were going to hold us over?"

"I feel you, bro. When is the shipment?"

"Tuesday at 9:30 pm on dock 27."

"Fuck it. Let's get this money."

"That's what the fuck I'm talking about. Let's eat, baby." Cash dapped Big Apple up as a sign of happiness.

***

Detective Boatman was sitting at his desk when his phone rang. He put his coffee down and picked it up. "Detective Boatman speaking, how may I help you?"

"On 127th, there's a light skin nigga name Freestyle. He got tattoos on his face with black locs. He have two kilos of cocaine in his bookbag and a black 9-millimeter on him, That's your weak link. Remember our fucking agreement, cop." Showtime hung up the phone after saying that.

Detective Boatman jumped up from his desk and ran out of the doors of the police station. It took him 25 minutes to get to 127th Street. He parked his car and called for backup once he seen Freestyle walking out of the pizza store. He opened his car door and looked dead at him. Freestyle saw him looking at him and he took off running, dropping his pizza and all.

"Freestyle, don't do it to yourself," Detective Boatman said as he took off after him, full force. One of the blue and whites seen him, waited for the right time and tackled Freestyle down to the ground. He put his gun to the back of his head. "Don't fucking move."

Freestyle closed his eyes as they picked him up off the ground. Detective Boatman looked at him then looked in the bookbag and saw the two kilos of cocaine. As the blue and white officer had his gun in his hand, Detective Boatman walked up to him and said, "You know you done fucked up right. Let's get hm down to the station, and hey thanks for the help."

"No problem, Detective."

The only question Detective Boatman said to himself was how did Showtime know he had all of this on him and why he ain't take him out himself?

***

Freestyle sat at the desk handcuffed with a 1000 thoughts going through his mind. Detective Boatman walked in the investigation room and looked at him with a folder in his hand. He placed the folder down on the table and sat down across from him.

"Let's talk. Two kilos of cocaine and a loaded 9-millimeter. Two-time felon. First, let's do the math. 5 years for the gun, 12 rounds a year for each bullet. That's 12 years plus the two kilos of cocaine. 20 on each one of them, that's 57 years you are looking at. Plus, you are a two time loser.

That's life. So, you are looking at life plus 57 years in prison or I can make all of this go away. I will walk you right out of them front doors. I don't want you, Freestyle. I want the bigger fish, Cash or Big Apple. I know you rep Browns. What it stand for again? Let me think. Oh yeah, Believe Real Ones Will Never Snitch. Let me tell you this, if you think or believe them real ones are going to hold you down, you will be a damn fool. What you need to think about is your little girl, sick mother and little brother. Your mother not going to make it, your little girl and brother will be in the system. You have to make a hard choice today, your family or the gang? I'll be back in two hours. I'm let you think about that. I'll bring you some food when I come back and when I walk in that door, I just want a yes or no, Freestyle."

Detective Boatman walked out the room, leaving Freestyle in his own thoughts at the desk. Detective Boatman walked up to Captain Moore, as she looked through the investigation window.

"Do you think you going to break him?"

"I already did."

Chapter 20

Cash pulled his car over and looked at Big Apple as he checked his gun. He made sure he had one in the head, as Big Apple checked his.

"It's 1 million and 73 G's in that bag homie, you ready?"

Yeah, let's get this shit out the way."

"Already." Cash put the car in drive, as they pulled up on the docks. Carlos had 10 heavy armed men standing around with M16 and AR-15s. It was dark on the docks, just two dim lights were on. Carlos was standing in the office as two of his guards brought Cash and Big Apple to him. Detective Boatman and 20 other officers and the SWAT team were all on the other side of the docks, watching everything play by play. That's when he saw Carlos place the bag on the table, open it up and saw all the kilos of cocaine. "That's it, boys. Let's rock and roll."

"Carlos, that's why I fuck with you because you know how to do business." Big Apple placed the money on the table.

That's when you heard all the gunshots.

"What the fuck. It's the police." Big Apple looked out the window. That's when Cash saw Carlos point his gun at Big Apple's head. Cash pushed Big Apple out the way as he pulled his gun out and shot Carlos two times in the chest, killing him. It was an all-out shootout. Big Apple picked the duffle bags up with the cocaine and ran out the back of the office, along with Cash. Carlos men were shooting it out with the police. They was so focused on the raid that they didn't even see when Carlos was shot by Cash.

"Bro, wait here. I'm going to go get the car. I'ma be right back," Cash said. Cash watched as the shootout was taking place. He ran to the side of his car and went to jump in when an officer jumped on him from behind. Cash rolled over on his back and put his gun to the officer's stomach and pulled the trigger. As he was pushing the cop off of him, he went to get up and was shot in the back shoulder. He hurried up, got in the car and peeled off. He made it to Big Apple. Big Apple jumped in the car as it was getting shot at. The back windows was shot out. Cash crashed through the gate and was gone,

"What the fuck? How they knew we was going to be there?" Big Apple said.

"I don't fucking know but we got the fuck up out of there and that's all that fucking matters. You got the money?"

"Hell no. I got the work. 50 bricks."

"We got to park the car and get the fuck up out of it now."

Captain Moore walked up to Detective Boatman as she looked around the scene. "What a fucking mess out here. What we got, Boatman?"

"Six dead shooters, plus Carlos Ganzellis and over a million in cash. Plus, a shitload of cocaine. Looks to be about 200 bricks and one wounded officer."

"Okay, what about Cash? Can any of this stick on him?"

"No. We don't got him on camera doing anything. Honestly, we can't even see his face."

"Fuck it. This right here was big, really big. I guess that get out of jail Freestyle told you about was worth it."

"Yeah, but Cash is still on my hitlist."

"Mine too. Get me a full report on my desk in the morning."

"Will do."

"Good job again, Detective," Captain Moore said as she walked off.

***

Nobody said a word as Rip and SB drove Big Apple and Cash back to the spot. SB burned the BMW, and broke out the ignition as if the car was stolen. Once back at the warehouse, SB helped Cash out of the SUV as Big Apple and Rip placed the bricks down on the table. Cash took his shirt off and Rip looked at his arm and shoulder.

"You good, doggy. It went in and out. That shit is going to hurt like hell the next few days though."

"I can take the pain. It's just another battle wound. What I want to know is how the fuck they knew we was going to be there? That was a set up to the fullest."

"Real talk. That shit got ugly real fast. Once Carlos placed that duffle bag on the table, them doors was being kicked in," Big Apple said.

"Look, I don't give a fuck what nobody say. Someone tipped the police off about that meeting tonight," SB walked up and said.

"Look, shit is ugly right now. I'm about to hit the block to see what the streets are taking about. Rip come with me."

"Yeah, I got you, bro."

"When y'all hear something, let me know what the fuck y'all hear."

"I copy that."

"Cash, good looking too. If you ain't push me out the way, I would have been bodied."

"Already, family."

Chapter 21

Symone walked up to Big Apple as he was overseeing the females bag up the cocaine.

"Big Apple, I need to tell you something."

Big Apple walked off from the girls, puffing his blunt.

"What's up, Symone?"

"I don't know how true it is, but I just got word that Freestyle got locked up a few days ago and he had 2 kilos of cocaine and his gun on him."

"Ain't no way he got caught with all of that and he still on the block. You know what? I'ma check that shit out and see what I come up with."

"Cool, I was just letting you know the word on the street."

"Good looking on that, little homie."

When Symone walked off, Big Apple thought back how Cash did front the homie 2 birds. He did walk in the room on the conversation the other day about the drop and pick up. Shit do add up but he just had to double check to make sure his facts was right.

***

Gangstar walked up to Showtime as he was sitting on his hood of the car, smoking a blunt as the music was playing.

"How you holding up, homie?"

"Shit I'm living day by day. You know how shit is."

"Yeah, I do. Don't think we going to let that shit ride because we not. As soon as shit cool down, we are going to roll them nigga. On the set, we ain't letting this shit ride."

"Gangstar, my moms been dead for over 3 weeks now. You talking about we ain't letting this shit ride. What the fuck you call it then?"

"Bro with these serial killings and gang shootouts, the police is heavy on the block right now. We trying to roll those niggas, not get booked at the same time. Real talk."

Showtime looked at his phone as it was going off and seen it was a private number calling him.

"Yo Gangstar, I have to take this call. I'll pull up on you in a minute."

Gangstar just nodded as Showtime got in his car and pulled off.

***

Freestyle walked into the warehouse up to Cash and dapped him up.

"Freestyle, what's the word? Where you been at the last few days? Bro, we could have used you around here."

"Just trying to make shit happen. Putting some shit together, that's all."

"Word. Word, I feel you on that shit. You heard about what happened to me and Big Apple and how I had to put Carlos down?"

"Hell naw what went down? When this shit happened?"

"It's crazy that you ask that. Not even two days after you got jammed up with them two kilos and that gun. How the fuck you get up out of that anyway?"

Freestyle looked at the door. That's when Big Apple place the gun to the back of his head.

"Thing about it nigga and I'll paint the walls with your blood. Fucking rat!"

"Yo Cash, Big Apple, it's nothing like that. Real talk."

"Well, tell me what's it's like motherfucker."

Before he could say anything, Cash looked at Symone and nodded. Symone walked up to Freestyle with her butterfly knife, slit his throat and watched as he fell down to his knees and. He bled out on the floor.

"Symone, his blocks are yours now," Cash said before walking off.

SB, Ray-J, and Rip all just looked at Freestyle's dead body on the floor, eyes open and looking into space with blood covering his hands from when he grabbed his throat.

***

Captain Moore walked out to the far end of the police station where the other officers were. When she got there, she looked down at Freestyle's dead body with his tongue pulled through his neck. She turned around and looked at Detective Boatman and said, "I guess someone figured it out. He was your CI so this is your mess to clean up."

With nothing else to be said, she turned around and walked off. Detective Boatman looked around one more time before shaking his head and saying Cash's name. He knew this blood was on Cash's hands.

Chapter 22

"This is what I need to get clear because Freestyle's dead body was at the far end of the police station last night. I need to make sure you ain't let nobody know from Browns that he was a rat." Detective Boatman looked at Showtime as they stood next to the Hudson River.

"You think I'm going to talk to them niggas after they killed my mother. News flash Detective, Cash is smart as fuck. I'm willing to bet he put 2 and 2 together about that shit. But I did my part. What's up with your end of the deal?"

"Keep your line open tonight. When I call you, don't pick up, just meet me at the abandoned warehouse off of 42nd Street."

"I'll be there."

"Good and remember this shit we got going on ain't over till I put the cuffs on Cash. Do I make myself clear?"

"No, this shit ain't over until those niggas is dead just like my fucking mother."

"I'll be in touch," Detective Boatman said as he walked off leaving Showtime standing there smoking a cigarette.

***

Ray-J walked with Symone on Lincoln Ave. She waited on him as he walked into the deli. She stood outside smoking a blunt, when she saw Gangstar's car riding by. He looked at her and they caught eye contact. He did a U-turn and pulled up in the front of the store with Money in the car. They both stepped out of the car and Symone pulled her gun out.

"Fuck up and die. Y'all niggas try me if y'all want and I swear I'ma clap one of y'all niggas."

"You got heart because you have a little pow pow on you now," Money said.

"Just like I flatlined that nigga Killer-B. When y'all niggas run up on me, ain't shit change. Money run up and I'm going to blast this bitch."

Gangstar pulled his gun out and looked at Symone. "Bitch you thought they stop making guns when they made yours. I run this shit. You know that, bitch."

Ray-J looked out of the deli window and seen what was going on. He pulled his gun out and walked out of the door next to Symone.

"What's up? We got a fucking problem here, because I ain't with the chit-chat."

Gangstar saw the police coming down the road. "I'll see y'all babies real soon. Come on, Money, let's get the fuck out of here."

"Yeah, do that, nigga, before y'all be a fucking crime scene."

Gangstar pulled off as Ray-J and Symone walked into the deli before the police pulled up. The owner of the deli let them out of the back of the store with their guns at hand.

***

Showtime looked at his watch. It was 12am. Detective Boatman called him at 11:30 pm and told him to go to the warehouse. When he looked, he saw the white lights from the car pulling up. Detective Boatman stepped out of the car, popped the trunk and pulled SB out. He was tied up as he fell on the ground.

"Make sure this nigga is dead. We don't need him coming back talking, Showtime. He was the one who took your mother. A neighbor gave us his description.

"You got my word that tonight is his last night breathing."

Detective Boatman got back in his car and drove off

"It's just me and you now, nigga. My mother blood is on your hands?" Showtime asked as he had the gun to SB face.

"Nigga fuck that bitch."

Showtime smacked SB in the face with the gun three times, knocking him to the ground.

"Her blood is on your hands, nigga. You know what the fuck happens when you are a part of this life," SB said as he was spitting up blood and teeth.

"Yeah, I know what type of life I live. That's why you should know you are not going to make it out of here alive."

"Nigga I done seen everything but the devil. Suck my dick. Do what the fuck you do."

Showtime pointed the gun at SB face and shot him two times in the head, killing him.

"Just know, you are the first of many bodies, nigga."

Chapter 23

Detective Boatman walked up to Detective Cross as he was leaning on his police car, smoking a cigarette.

"It's good to have you back, Cross."

"Yeah, it's good to be back, especially for days like this."

"Yeah, I know. What we got here?"

"Two elderly couples killed, beaten to death in the worst way. Our suspect changed their mind but this just don't make any sense to me. This is the tenth killing from this serial killer, but there is no motive of why they are killing people, and why this couple? Why kill them the way they did?"

"One think I know Cross is you are a damn good detective. You are going to figure it out. People like this serial killer always slip up somewhere."

"Yeah, but how many more people are going to be killed before he or she slips up is the question?"

"Come on, let's go over the crime scene again. You might have missed something."

"Yeah, a fresh set of eyes would be good."

***

Showtime laid on his bed, thinking to himself. He thought killing SB was going to make him feel better but it was just like killing any other nigga. The only difference was he knew SB had his mother's blood on his hands. He made a deal with the police. He sold his soul. He could never be a real nigga again. Even if nobody ever found out, he would always know, and that's something he would always have to live with. He made up his mind that being a real nigga is just too hard nowadays.

***

"Ray-J, what happened the other day with you and Symone?"

"Gangstar rolled up holding his heat, just talking shit. I would have popped his ass but 12 was coming down the block. We got the fuck on out of there."

"We can't allow disrespect like that. Get up with SB, go shoot that nigga spot u and tag Browns."

"Yo, I been calling SB for the last few days. That man phone been going to voicemail. He's been MIA."

"Yeah, something just don't feel right about that to me at all. Get up with Rip and I'll try to find SB."

"Say less, I'll get on that tonight, Cash."

Ray-J walked off to let Rip know tonight they had to stand on business. Whoever was outside, they name was on the grocery list.

***

Gangstar had his eyes closed as he was getting his manhood sucked on. He loved the feeling of having his dick in a pretty female's mouth as her tongue licked all over his balls. He started to fuck her mouth harder and harder. Then, he stopped because he heard the sound of gunshots going off. He pushed her to the side and jumped up. He grabbed his gun and went to run out of the room, when he heard Money yell, "Get down. Get down."

Ray-J and Rip stood in front of the house, shooting M16 and AR-15s. They were shooting all the windows out as Symone tagged the cars and streets with one word. Browns.

"Man fuck this," Gangstar said as he jumped up shooting out the window.

Rip yelled, "The back window."

Gangstar ducked down as bullets sprayed through the window. That's when you heard the sound of car tires peeling off. Gangstar ran to the front door just in time to see the car lights turn the corner. He went back in the house. Money was getting off the floor and so were two more other people. He walked to the back bedroom to see shorty lying dead in a pool of blood on the bed. She was shot in the chest. Gangstar closed her eyes and bit down on his teeth when seeing that. He was knowing Symone told them about the spot because she knew where it was at.

Chapter 24

"What we got here, Boatman?" Detective Cross asked as he looked around the crime scene at all the blue and white police cars and people standing around.

"Alex Bird, age 26 AKA SB, shot 2 times in the head is the cause of death. He was a member of the Browns crew off of Al Bundy Ave and Smith Street."

"The backlash that's going to come behind this one. You know how these gangs get down already."

"Yeah, I do. That's why I'm going to go have a talk with Cash today to try and stop what's about to happen."

"You need me to come?"

"No, just wrap this up for me. That's all."

"No problem. I got you."

"Thanks, Cross. I appreciate you, buddy."

"That's what I'm here for."

Detective Boatman walked to his car. He knew he had to have a sit down with Cash, but he ain't give two fucks if they crew killed each other. He just had to make it look good for his job. Fuck Browns, fuck Cash. Shit, fuck Gangstar and Showtime. That's how he felt.

***

Showtime walked into the house and looked around at all the broken glass and bullet holes everywhere. Gangstar looked at him as he walked into the house.

"What the fuck happened here?"

"What the fuck it look like? Niggas came through blasting last night and we got a dead body in the back room still. Look Showtime, I know you got a lot going on right now but I need your head in the game. We are at war and we are fucking losing right now."

"My head is in the game bro."

"Good because you, Money and Solid is going to spray these niggas shit back up tonight. We going to let them know we ain't laying down for no fucking body at all."

"Say less. I'm on it." Showtime looked at Money and Solid as they moved the dead body out the back room. He turned around and walked out of the front door, mind ready for war but this had been personal to him since his mother was killed.

***

Detective Boatman opened the doors to the pool hall. He looked dead at Cash as he walked up to him.

"New York finest, what the fuck do I owe the pleasure?"

"I'm trying to stop these bodies from falling. There's been a killing last night."

"Well Detective, I ain't have nothing to do with nobody's being dropped last night."

"Yeah, I know this one ain't have nothing to do with you. That's why I'm here, Cash."

"What are you talking about?"

"See for yourself." Detective Boatman passed Cash a folder with pictures inside of SB dead in the back of an abandoned building. Cash bit down on his teeth and closed his eyes as he handed back the file to Detective Boatman.

"Do you know anybody who would want to have him killed?"

"No I don't, Detective."

"Here's my card if you think of anything." Detective Boatman placed his card on the counter and walked off. He ain't give a fuck about SB. He just wanted the pleasure of looking at Cash's face when he told him the news that one of his shooters was dead. What gave it more pleasure was that it was because of him that he was dead.

Chapter 25

Money walked into the room where Gangstar was at. Gangstar was cleaning his gun as he was smoking a cigarette.

"Big bro, can I have a word with you?" Gangstar placed his gun down and puffed on his cigarette before talking.

"Yeah, what's popping, little homie?"

"Real talk, we been dropping bodies and losing bodies since this war started and it was all over Tigger and a dice game. Tigger rolled a nigga for a half of bird. We done lost 50 birds and $300,000 in cash. Plus, someone bodied the plug and we still don't know the ends and outs of that. All I'm saying is that we really just need to accept our losses and get this money again. That's all, big homie."

Gangstar nodded. "Yeah, I was thinking about that last night, but you do know if we don't strike back, this will be a loss on our end, right? You know how that shit will make us look."

"Man, fuck how it look right now. All we need to worry about is this money and real talk, this dude Showtime been moving weird as fuck lately."

"Yeah, I been seeing that, real talk. Look, have Solid keep an eye on him and go to the pool hall and let Cash know I want to have a conversation with him at his place of choice."

"Say less, I'm on that shit now."

Gangstar respected Money. He was about his business and he was loyal as fuck.

***

"There's only one way for me to say this, the homie SB was bodied. I don't know when. Two shots to the dome. His body was found behind the old run-down abandoned buildings. We know who blood is on his hands."

Ray-J shook his head and so did Rip. Big Apple puffed on his blunt as Cash was talking. Symone looked to the left and seen Money walking up to the pool hall doors. She pulled her gun out on him.

"Yo Cash, check it out."

Cash looked and pulled his gun out. "This little nigga must have a death wish pulling up over here."

Money walked inside. Cash and Big Apple walked up to him.

"Nigga you ready to stop fucking breathing?" Big Apple said.

"I ain't even come looking for no smoke. I just got a message. That's all."

"What the fuck is this message?"

"Gangstar wants to meet up with you Cash. You pick the time and place."

Cash looked at Big Apple. Big Apple nodded.

"Coney Island, tomorrow noon, by the ice cream shop."

"Say less. I'll let him know."

"Let his ass know don't be late. This is the only time this genie is coming out of this bottle."

Money nodded and walked out the doors to his car.

***

"Gangstar, I know you can't be fucking serious right now. You must have lost your fucking marbles."

"Look, I know you ain't trying to hear what I'm about to say, but we got to think about the bigger picture right now."

"Nigga fuck the bigger picture. Fuck what you talking about, you soft hearted ass nigga. I'm done with this clown ass shit. You talking about a bigger picture but my mother is in a fucking grave. Fuck you. Fuck this hood. I'm done, nigga."

Showtime pulled his flag off, threw it on the floor, turned around and walked off.

Gangstar yelled out to him as he walked off. "If you do this, ain't no coming back."

"Nigga fuck what you talking about and fuck this hood." Showtime ain't say another word as he walked out of the doors. He was knowing that when this is said and done, he's going to have a bullet for Gangstar ass too, on his dead mother's grave. He promised himself that.

Chapter 26

Cash's black Range Rover pulled up. Cash, Big Apple, Symone and Rip stepped out. Gangstar, Money, and Solid was standing next to the ice cream shop when Cash and his crew walked up on them. Gangstar nodded at Cash. Him and Cash walked off where nobody could hear them talk.

"You called this meeting. I'm here what you have to put on the table," Cash spoke.

"A truce. Let's end this war. You keep your people on your side and I'll do the same. I respect your blocks and you respect mine."

"You know all of this started because one of your hittas bodied one of mine because he lost a few dollars on a dice game. Then, he stole a half of brick from my runner."

"Everybody is dead, Cash. Look around, it's just me and you standing here right now. The police breathing down both our necks over water under the bridge."

"The two blocks that a neutral zones where our corners meet, are my blocks now. That's the only way this shit going to work."

"And why you get them blocks?"

"To show my crew this war wasn't for nothing and off GP for your man killing my little hitta. That sparked this war."

"Respect. I'll give you that. One more thing."

"And what's that?"

"Showtime ain't a part of my crew no more. So, what he do ain't on us."

"We can deal with that nigga."

"So, we good?"

"Yeah." Gangstar put his hand out there to shake Cash's. Cash shook his hand to seal the deal. Both of them nodded and walked off. Showtime was in the cut watching it all, mad as fuck. Niggas wanted to double cross him, so we was going to triple cross everybody.

***

"What you got here, Detective Cross?" Detective Boatman asked him.

"A map of where all the serial killings were at and they all are 20 minutes away from each other in a circle if you can tell."

"I see that. So, our suspect is killing where they are the most comfortable at."

"Yeah, and each killing is three weeks apart from the last one."

"But I'll get back to this later. Tell me what you got for me because I know you came down here for a reason."

"Yeah, my CI just told me that the Go-Gettas and Browns crew just had a meeting and they ending this war."

"Did he tell you who was the one who called this meeting? Who reached out first?"

"No, he ain't get into all those details, but he did tell me about a shooting the other night and a female was killed in the shooting."

"She was shot in the chest. Let me guess."

"I don't know if she was shot in the chest, but didn't we have a Jane Doe whose body was found the other day with a cause of death of gunshot wound?"

"Boatman, I love how you put shit together. Should we go pay Gangstar a little visit?" "I think we should."

"Let's go then."

Chapter 27

Showtime was sitting on the hood of his car in the back alley next to the burned down apartments. When Detective Boatman pulled up on hir, he stepped out of his car and walked up on him.

"What's up man? What's this shit about now?" Showtime asked.

"You know the deal we made. Its's time for you to come up with some more information." Showtime nodded "And it's time for you to bring me another nigga body, too."

"In due time, what you got for me?"

"Word is that Cash got a warehouse off of Avon Ave where he keep all his drugs at money and guns. Now, I never been there, but my source told me that's where he keep all his shit at."

"How reliable is your source?"

"My source is one hundred. Trust that."

Solid had been following Showtime all day. He was standing next to a dumpster listening to everything. Showtime never seen him. Detective Boatman pulled his sunglasses off to wipe the dirt off of them. That's when he seen Solid in the reflection on the sunglasses, standing behind the dumpster. He looked at Showtime.

"You really need to watch who following you, because it could cost both of us big time."

Showtime didn't understand what Detective Boatman was talking about.

Detective Boatman turned around real fast and started shooting at the dumpster. Solid jumped from behind the dumpster and took off running. Showtime cut him off and started shooting at him. Solid got shot in the leg and fell down. Showtime walked up to him.

"Showtime, what the fuck you doing, bro?"

Detective Boatman walked up to them.

"So, Gangstar got you following me?"

"No bro. You tripping. We better than this."

Showtime pointed his gun at Solid's face.

"No we not. Remember you wanted the peace treaty after they killed my mother."

Before Solid could say anything, Showtime shot him two times in the face, killing him.

"Next time, make sure no one is following your ass. I'm not going down because you are being sloppy. Don't make me tie up all loose ends, including your ass." Detective Boatman said as he walked off.

Showtime looked at Solid one more time before walking off as well. Once both of them were gone, a local crackhead named Know It All moved the blanket that was covering the shopping cart that he was hiding behind. Through the holes in the blanket, he saw it all and heard it all. He looked at Solid and pushed his cart from over there before they came back.

***

Know It All walked up Bronx Boulevard, right up to Symone where she was on the block talking to one of her homegirls.

Symone looked at him. "What you want?"

"I need to speak to Cash."

"About what?"

"About the word on the block."

"So tell me, what's the word on the block?"

"Tell Cash if he wants to know the word on the block reach out to me. Better sooner than later." Know It All went to walk off when Symone called him back.

"Hold on, let me call Cash."

After a few seconds, Symone was walking Know It All to the back where Cash was at. Cash pulled his blunt and walked up to Know It All.

"Know It All, my beautiful diamond said you had to tell me something. So, tell me what's the word on the block."

"You know that kid's mother who got killed. He's not living right. He's not living by the code of the streets."

"And what you mean by that?"

"He was talking to a Detective Boatman about your warehouse and all the drugs and money in there off of Avon Ave. He got a source that told him the shit is over there."

Cash walked up to Know It All and grabbed him by the shirt and placed his gun to his head.

"How the fuck I know you ain't the source? How I know you wasn't talking to the Detective and now you just over here trying to get your next high, nigga."

"I can prove it. That's how."

Cash let him go. "How the fuck you going to prove it, nigga?"

"Because Showtime killed Solid because Solid caught him talking to the cop. I was hidden behind my cart. I seen it all and the detective told Showtime don't make him clean up all loose strings, including him. The body still there behind the burned down apartments."

Cash looked at Ray-J and Rip. "Yo y'all, go check that shit out and see if there is a body behind there. Y'all know how Solid looks. Matter fact, Symone you go with Ray-J. Rip go start cleaning the warehouse out. I'll have Big Apple meet you over there. Know It All going to stay right here with me until I hear from you, Ray-J."

"Cool, I'm going to get on that now."

"Call me as soon as you see the body."

"Copy that." Cash watched as everyone left the spot. He looked at Know It All and passed him a cigarette to smoke while they waited.

***

"Detective Cross, look at the front of the house."

"Yeah, you can tell this house been shot up. You can tell whoever was here is long gone now."

"Should we go inside and check it out?"

"Why not. We are already here."

"Good point."

Both Detectives walked into the house, guns out looking around the place. Detective Boatman walked to the back room.

"Say Cross, come check this out." When Detective Cross walked to the back room, he saw all the blood on the bed.

"I guess we know where she was killed at now."

"Call this in and let's get CSI down here now."

"Let's do that, Boatman." Detective Cross looked around some more at all the shells on the floor.

***

Ray-J looked down at Solid's dead body. He then called Cash and after a few seconds, Cash picked up.

"Talk to me."

"The crackhead wasn't lying. This nigga is dead dead. Shot a few times like he was trying to run and got hit up."

"Cool, get the fuck up out of there now, and meet Rip at the warehouse."

"Copy that."

Cash hung up the phone and looked at Know It All.

"I guess you were telling the truth. So, Showtime is a rat now. What you trying to get out of all of this shit?"

"I'm just trying to get high and some money to eat with. That's all."

"You know what? I can do that. You came thru for me."

Cash reached in his pocket, pulled out two one hundred dollar bills and passed them to Know It All. He then handed him six grams of crack.

"Now, this is our personal conversation. I don't want to hear this again."

"You have my word that you won't."

"Good. The door is that way." Cash watched as he left. He then pulled his phone out and made a call.

Chapter 28

Detective Boatman waited under the train tracks for Cash to pull up. That's when he seen the blue lights coming from the BMW pulling up. Cash stopped his car, stepped out and walked up to Detective Boatman as he puffed on a cigar.

"And what do I owe the pleasure of this phone call, Cash?"

"You keep trying to fuck my shit up, Detective. I'm going to fuck your shit over. You got your own personal problems you need to deal with."

"First of all, you could never fuck my personal shit up and what problems are you talking about?"

"For one, that body you need to clean up, because I'm pretty sure your footprint will match that footprint in the dirt. Two, all my shit is out of that warehouse, so don't waste your taxpayers' money and man hours on a raid. Look at your facial expression. You trying to figure out how I know all of this shit. Let me drop another diamond on you. Showtime is a rat but not one of your loose ends. Like I said, next time you try to fuck my shit up, I'm going to fuck all your shit up, cop." Cash puffed on his cigar, got back in his car and drove off, leaving Detective Boatman in his thoughts.

Detective Boatman got into his car trying to figure out how the fuck did Cash know all of this. He stopped at the red light. He looked on the corner at Know It All. He then paid more attention to his shopping cart and the blanket. Then, he thought back and remembered seeing the cart where he and Showtime were standing at.

"Fuck, that's how Cash knew it was me. That fucking bum. Don't worry, I have a trick for his ass real soon. Fucking snitch." Detective Boatman pulled his phone out and made a call to Showtime.

***

Big Apple walked up to Money in front of Gangstar's barbershop. Money looked at him as if he was crazy. "You must be lost or something."

Big Apple smiled. "Go get your boss. I need to talk with him, now."

"Wait here." Money walked off. A few seconds later, Money walked right back up on Big Apple. "He said come inside." Money walked him to the room on the left where Gangstar was at.

Gangstar nodded at Money. Money turned around and walked off.

"What's up? What can I do for you?"

"We have a big fucking problem."

"And what's this big fucking problem that we are having?"

"Showtime is a fucking rat, and he killed Solid with the crooked ass Detective Boatman."

"And why should I believe you?"

"One, I ain't coming down here on good faith. Two, I have proof."

"What's your proof?"

Big Apple pulled his phone out and showed him the picture of Solid's dead body.

Gangstar closed his eyes when he seen that.

"Like I said he's a fucking rat and he told the boys where we keep our work. I don't know how he found out, but he did."

Gangstar nodded before talking, "I'll take care of it myself."

"Good." Big Apple got up and walked out the room.

A few seconds later, Money walked into the room.

"Yo, when was the last time you talked to Solid?"

"Early today. He said he was following Showtime into the burned down apartments."

"You talk to him since?"

"No. I called him a few times. He ain't pick up."

"That's because he's dead and Showtime is a rat. It's time for Showtime to see his mother."

"Fucking right."

***

Know It All was sleeping in his boxes on the side of the building when Showtime walked up on him. Showtime looked around and moved the blanket off the front of the box. Know It All looked at Showtime as Showtime pulled his gun out and pointed it at his face.

"Sometimes it's not good to Know It All."

Before Know It All could say a word, Showtime shot him two times in the face, killing him. He then turned around and walked off.

Chapter 29

Detective Cross looked at his watch. It was 9:30 pm. He took the last shot of gin he had in his shot glass and got up to leave out of the bar. He waved to everyone as he was leaving. He walked to his truck in the parking lot and got inside. That's when he heard the sound of a gun clicking in the back of his head.

"Don't do nothing shady. Just hear what the fuck I got to say and I'll be on my way. Don't worry, I'm not going to shoot you in the back. I'm going to shoot you in the head. I know you like to wear vests. Now, keep your hands on the steering wheel and I'll be on my way after I say what I have to say, understood?"

"Yeah, speak your peace."

"Detective Boatman ain't who you think he is, or his CI. They work together on more than you know. Behind the burnt down apartments, there's a body. He was shot and killed. Detective Boatman knows this, matter fact, he was there when it happened. I'm willing to bet you if you look at the shoe print in the dirt over there, Detective Boatman's footprint will match it. Also, check the bullet shells to see if his gun is a match to one of them."

"Why are you telling me this?"

"Because just maybe your shooting was a warning to him. The body been there for two days now. Have a goodnight, detective and next time lock your doors. Don't take your hands off the wheel for three minutes. If you do, you will regret it."

Detective Cross closed his eyes as they got out the SUV. He did what they said until the three minutes was up. Then, he drove off.

***

Detective Cross pulled up to the burned down apartments. He stepped out of his SUV, pulled his gun out and walked behind the building. He stopped when he saw a leg. He walked a little bit closer and saw Solid's dead body lying there. He pulled his phone out and called it in. Within 45 minutes, you had 20 plus officers on the scene and CSI down there as well. Captain Moore walked up to Detective Cross.

"How the hell did you come across this body, Cross?"

"Would you believe me if I told you someone put a gun to the back of my head and told me where to find it?"

Before the Captain could respond, one of the CSI workers called out to them.

"Excuse me, Captain. Detective, we have another bod over here."

Both of them looked at each other and walked off to where the body was. Detective Cross shook his head.

"Do you know who this is, Cross?"

"Yes I do, Captain. They call him Know It All and for him to be murdered, he must have knew something."

"Your bodies, your case. Get on it."

"Yes ma'am."

Detective Cross knew that Detective Boatman would be his number one suspect. Shit didn't add up and he was going to get to the bottom of it.

Chapter 30

Two Weeks Later

"Captain Moore, can I have a word with you?"

"Sure what is it, detective? What do you have for me so far?"

"Nothing much but I have a feeling that all the shooting and murders are all coming from one gang."

"And what gang is this?"

"Because Showtime is the main one with nothing to lose. I found a fingerprint on Know It All's box that belong to him and if I'm right, the same man that killed the guy in the alley was the same one to kill Know It All. That shooter is Showtime."

"And let me guess you need a warrant to raid the house where the Go Gettas be?"

"In a nutshell, yes I do."

"Okay, detective, you have your warrant. Don't come back empty handed."

"I won't, Captain." Detective Moore walked off knowing shit was about to hit the fan. Not just with the Go-Gettas but with Detective Boatman too.

***

Gangstar walked into the kitchen as he watched Money and four more of his homies break down three kilos of cocaine to make them into six. They was just really getting back on their feet from fronting 40 birds from the plug to pay Cash and his crew for Showtime's family. That was a big blow for them. The only good part was that the plug was killed in the raid so their debt was dead. Shit was still hard, grinding back up from all the losses they been taking back to back.

"How we looking over here, playboy?"

"This shit is like butter. We flipped 3 into 6 with no problem. I'm ready to hit the block and get this baby love."

"So, let's bag this shit up and get this money."

"Real talk."

Gangstar looked at the door. All you heard was a big explosion, the front door getting blown off the hinges and the police yelling freeze freeze. Gangstar pulled his gun out and started shooting at the police along with Money and the others. One of the crew threw the kilos into a trash bag and took off running when he was shot in the back. Money turned around and was shot three times in the chest. Gangstar grabbed the bag and ran out of the back door. There was police there too. He shot one of them in the neck, killing him. He dropped the bag with the kilos inside and ran to the far end of the yard. He jumped over the gate and by the time the police got to the gate, he was gone out of sight.

"What we got, detective?"

"We have 5 dead bodies, 6 kilos of cocaine and about $100,000 in money, Captain."

"Don't forget one dead officer on our end. Get everything tagged and bagged up. I have to call someone's wife and mother and let them know they son and husband was killed on the job today."

"Yes ma'am." Captain Moore walked off as Detective Boatman walked into the house.

"Hey Cross, why you ain't tell me you was raiding the Go-Gettas. I would have helped you out."

"It was a last-minute thing. Hey, I have some things I need to get done for the captain," Detective Cross said as he walked off, not saying nothing else to Detective Boatman. He knew he was just as dirty as the motherfuckers he was after.

Chapter 31

Cash was watching the news when he seen the Go-Gettas spot being raided. He puffed on his blunt and said to himself.

"I told you that boy Showtime was a rat. Now look at you, the whole crew is dead and you are on the run for murdering a cop. Nigga your career is over."

That's when Symone walked into the room.

"Yo, check the news out. It's over for that boy."

"Damn, that just happened?"

"Yeah, like two hours ago. Shit is super ugly for him right now. Facts."

"I'm glad I got the fuck away from them niggas."

"Me too, so what's up?"

"I just dropped that money off. I need a new re-up."

"Shit, no problem. Let's get that to you then." Symone looked at the news one more time before walking off, knowing one time that they was her family.

***

Gangstar walked to the back of the lake; it was dark outside. He looked and saw Showtime sitting on a boulder. Gangstar picked up a rock and threw it into the lake. He and Showtime used to come here all the time when they were younger and on the run. It was like the only place the police never looked at for them.

"Gangstar, how did it come to this, bro?"

100

"I been asking myself that all night. Showtime, the whole crew is dead, Money got killed by the police, so did Rightside, Hit-man and Paperboy. Symone killed Killed-B. I'm on the run for murdering a cop."

"I been thinking, bro. We can get shit back the way it used to be."

Gangstar looked at him when he said that. "How, Showtime? You don't think I know you killed Solid." At that time, Gangstar pulled his gun out and pointed it at Showtime's face.

"What the fuck did y'all expect? Y'all niggas left me," Showtime said with tears coming down his face.

"How the fuck did we leave you, bro? I gave up 10 kilos and fronted 40 from the plug for you and put up 300 large for your family. How the fuck did we leave you? That's over 2 million. That's love. That's loyalty."

"Fuck that, man. You made a pact with niggas that killed my mother."

"I was doing what I had to do for the family, the team. The gang was bigger than me and you. It was for all of us. I'm sorry about what happened to your mother, but you went against the family and started working with the police because you couldn't control your fucking emotions." Gangstar had tears coming down his face as he said that, looking at his childhood friend, his brother.

"This is how the fuck you going to do me? We go back to the sandbox," Showtime said, taking a deep breath.

"Now it's time to put you in the sandbox."

'I thought it was Go-Gettas for life. Me and you."

"I did too but remember you dropped your flag. Now, it's only me."

Gangstar had tears coming down his eyes as he pulled the trigger. All you heard was the sound of the blast from the Glock-40 going off in the night air and Showtime's body collapsed on the ground. Gangstar kissed his two fingers and placed then on Showtime cheek and said, "I love you nigga, but you brought this shit on yourself. Sleep in peace, homie. Go-Gettas for life."

Chapter 32

Detective Boatman walked up to Showtime's dead body and looked down at him with a single gunshot wound to the head.

"What we got here, Detective Boatman?"

"Jason Miller AKA Showtime. Some school kids came across his body this morning."

"Did you know him?"

"Yes, Captain. He was my CI."

Captain Moore took her pen out and moved Showtime's shirt, showing his gun.

"He had a pistol on him and never pulled it." Captain Moore called CSI over to them. "Tag this pistol and have a ballistic test done on it ASAP."

"Yes ma'am."

"Respectfully, I was going to have that done."

"I know you was but see when you said his street name, it rang a bell to me, and I remembered that Detective Cross came across his fingerprint at another crime scene with two homicides. I need to make sure his pistol isn't linked to that as well. We don't need Detective Cross chasing watches."

"No, we don't."

"Good that we are on the same page. Make sure you have a full report on my desk by tomorrow. No later than noon."

"10-4 ma'am." Detective Boatman bit down on his teeth as she walked away.

***

Detective Cross picked Detective Boatman's front door. He walked into his house and looked around. He made his way upstairs to his bedroom closet. He turned the light on and looked inside and saw all Detective Boatman shoes on the floor. He pulled out his LED light, turned off the closet light and went over all his shoes until he saw the blood on the side of a pair of black shoes. He pulled out his evidence bag and scrapped a few blood drops into the bag. He placed the bag into his pocket and did the same thing with another bag but this time it was dirt off the bottom of the shoe. After he was done, he placed the shoes back, closed the closet back and left out of the house. Once back at the station, he walked to the lab to see Kimberly.

"Hey Detective Cross, what can I do for you?"

"I need you to see if you can get a match on this blood from the Jane Doe case I'm working on."

"Sure thing. I guess you and the Captain are on a roll today."

"What do you mean?"

"She had me do a ballistic test on a gun and the bullet came back to 3 homicides. The same case you are working on."

"You got to be fucking kidding me. Where did she get the gun from?"

"A homicide. Some kids came across it. His name was Showtime. I remember hearing that name. I can't remember his government name."

"Kimberly, I have to go. Please call me when you find out the results."

"Will do so."

"Thanks." Detective Cross walked out the lab, hoping that he was wrong about Detective Boatman but if he wasn't he was going to wear them same silver cuffs. There was no getting around it.

***

"Captain, I just left Kimberly's lab. She told me that the gun that you had her do the ballistic test on came back a match on both homicides, ma'am."

"I had a feeling they were linked to that gun. So, we know who the shooter was."

"Yeah, we do. Now I just have to find out what Know It All knew that someone didn't want him to tell."

"Well find out and let the know something, detective."

"Will do, ma'am."

"10-4."

As Detective Cross was leaving the office, Kimberly called him. He closed the Captain's door before picking up the phone.

"Hey Kimberly. What you got for me?"

"The blood sample you brought me today was a match to the Jane Doe. You and the Captain are on a roll today."

"Yeah, you can say that."

"Just call me if you need me again."

"Will do." Detective Cross knew he had to go confront Detective Boatman even worse, arrest him.

Chapter 33

Detective Boatman walked up into Cash's pool hall. Cash looked at him as he walked in right up to the bar where Cash was.

"What the fuck do I owe the pleasure of this visit?"

"I'm trying to see what you know about Showtime being killed last night."

"What the fuck? That's news to my ears. You kidding me right? Someone done killed your rat. I'll think I'll have a drink to that."

"So, you don't know nothing about it?"

"Nigga you got me fucked up. I ain't no fucking rat. Fuck that dead boy."

"Make sure you keep that same energy, nigga because your house is about to crumble. I promise you that."

"If you are done with your threats, you can see yourself the fuck out of my spot."

"Don't worry. I'll see you real soon."

"Planning on it, cop."

Detective Boatman tapped the bar two times before walking out the pool hall.

***

Detective Cross pulled up under the train tracks where he knew Detective Boatman was going to be. He stepped out of the car and walked up to him.

"Cross, you don't never come down here. Something must be on your mind."

"It's over, Boatman. I put it all together, the murders and your part you played in them."

"I don't know what you are talking about, Cross. You might be barking up the wrong tree."

"I don't think I am. You were there the day Showtime killed Solid. You had blood on your shoe. You forget to clean them and Know It All saw what happened that day. That's why you had Showtime kill him. So your little dirty secret wouldn't come out. I did some investigation work and witnesses said that SB was arrested by a cop and wasn't seen no more. Showtime knew SB had his mother's blood on his hand so I'm thinking you picked SB up and brought him to Showtime. Am I getting hot yet? I put it together. There's nothing more I hate than a fucking dirty cop."

Detective Boatman clapped as he smiled. "So, you did some investigation work. So fuckin what! Big deal. Who the fuck is going to believe you? It's my word vs yours. A few scumbags got killed. Who gives a fuck? NYC is better off without them."

"Detective Boatman, you have the right to remain silent. Anything you say can and will be used against you in the court of law. Place your hands in the air. You are under arrest."

"You got to be fucking kidding me. Not today, nigga."

Detective Boatman pulled his gun out and shot two rounds at Detective Cross.

Detective Cross ducked down behind his squad car

"You know I'm deadly with these two Glock-9s, Cross. I call them my bitches."

"Well, you are going to die with your bitches in your hands." Detective Cross had his gun in his hand.

Detective Cross ran from behind his car shooting at Detective Boatman, hitting him in the shoulder but just a graze. Detective Boatman turned around and fired two shots at Cross, hitting him in the vest. Detective Cross fell backwards, dropping his gun. Boatman ran up on him and kicked him in the face, making him roll over on his back. He stood over top of him with his gun pointed at his face. Detective Boatman looked around to see if anybody was around. What he didn't see was Detective Cross press his radio button down, when Detective Boatman didn't see it.

"Now look at you, you done dropped your gun, trying to lock me up. Motherfucker do you think I'm let you lock me up?"

"What the fuck is going to be your story when they start asking questions about me?"

"I don't know. I'll think of something. Just like when I had Solid killed and Know It All along with SB. You should have saw his face when I dropped him off to Showtime. I was there when Solid got killed. Shit, I shot him in the leg and I stood right there when Showtime killed him. There might be some blood on my shoes but let me tell you what's going to happen now. I'm going to kill you go arrest Gangstar, have him shoot my gun that I kill you with. Then, I'm going to kill him and I will say something nice at your service, buddy. That sounds like a plan to me."

"Now, let me tell you my secret."

"Sure, go ahead. It ain't like nobody will ever know."

Detective Cross moved his arm and showed Detective Boatman he had the radio button pressed down. Then, he released it.

"No the fuck you didn't, you dirty motherfucker."

"Yeah, the fuck I did. Everybody heard you."

That's when you heard the Captain's voice.

"Boatman, we heard it all. It's over. You do that and it's the death sentence. That ain't the road you want to take. I have cars on the way to you right now. There's no getting out of this."

Detective Boatman looked and seen the police cars coming his way. He grabbed Detective Cross by the shirt and picked him up, using him as a shield as he started shooting at the police cars. Detective Cross punched him in the face to make him turn his attention off of the police. That's when a single gunshot went off, shooting Detective Boatman in the head, killing him. Detective Cross looked at him as he was catching his breath and shaking his head at Detective Boatman's dead body with the gun still in his hand.

Chapter 34

"Detective Cross, you did a good ass job out there today. I would have never put all that together. How did you do it?"

"I told you someone really put a gun to the back of my head and told me everything I told you the other day."

"You wasn't joking. You have to be fucking kidding me. Do you know who it was?"

"No, I don't."

"Well, I know you'll figure it out real soon. I'm sure of it."

"You know what Captain, to tell you the truth, I been shot 12 times. I had a gun put to the back of my head. I don't even know if I want to poke that bear no more. I'm just going to leave it alone because at the end of the day, Boatman is dead, Showtime is dead and our murders are solved. That's all that matters to me."

"Well if that works for you, then it works for me."

"Then it's nothing else to be said then."

Detective Cross knocked two times on the Captain's desk and walked out of her office. Captain Moore knew she couldn't reveal that she told Detective Boatman to do what he had to do, and she would cover it. She didn't know he was going to kill people or set them up. He did what she told him, and it cost him his life but when you live by the gun, you die by the gun. He died holding his gun. And that was a secret nobody would ever know. She was going to take it to the grave.

***

Symone stepped out of the car and walked into her spot. She turned the lights on and walked to her kitchen. She got some juice out of the fridge. When she turned around, Gangstar was standing there pointing a gun at her head. She was so shocked that she dropped the juice on the floor, breaking the bottle.

"How you knew I lived here?" She asked backing up.

"It don't matter. All that matters is that you cost me so much money, you disloyal bitch."

"How was I disloyal? I did shit for you that I would have never did for no one else."

"Showtime is dead because I killed him. He killed Solid, and you killed Killer-B. Now, you wearing these brown flags. This is a fucking spit in my face, bitch," he said as he grabbed her by the hair.

"They had me at fucking gunpoint with a shot gun to my fucking head. To hear you say fuck that bitch and then you hung up the phone. That was a spit in my fucking face. What happened to fucking loyalty? Go-Gettas ride or die. You left me for fucking dead with the wolves."

"You know how the fucking game goes." Gangstar pushed her and put the gun to her face as he had her hair in his other hand.

"I lost every fucking thing. Now I'm on the fucking run for murder. They calling me a cop killer. My pictures is all over the fucking news."

"That sound like a you problem." Symone looked at the glass on the counter. When Gangstar shook his head, she picked it up and smacked him in the face with it. He let her go. She took off running out of the house. Gangstar ran behind her, shooting at her.

Symone ducked down in someone's yard. Gangstar looked around and took off running when he ain't see her. A few seconds later, Symone came out. She looked at her arm where Gangstar shot her. She ran back into her house, got her car keys, got into her car and drove off, holding her shoulder.

Chapter 35

Captain Moore walked up to Detective Cross with a hurt look on her face. He placed his coffee down on the desk and looked at her. It was 9:25pm.

"Captain, what is that look on your face?" He asked puzzled.

"The serial killer struck again tonight." Detective Cross went to get up.

"Cross, sit down you can't work this case. It's more I have to tell you."

"What's up? Why can't I work this case?"

With a deep breath she said, "He murdered your wife and kids and set the house on fire. I just got the call. I'm so sorry."

Detective Cross took off running out of the police station to his car. It took him 35 minutes to get to his house. It was in full flame. He looked to the right and saw the body bags. He ran to them, fighting the police off of him. He opened it up to see his wife of 15 years dead with her throat cut wide open. He walked to the other body bags and seen his baby girl and baby boy with the same cut. He fell to his knees and started crying out of control, not believing what he was seeing. It took 4 officers to restrain him. Captain Moore walked up to him and hugged him as tears came out of her eyes. She watched his house in full flames just burn, Even though Cross was a detective, the laws of the streets say if you are not flying my colors, then you are a fucking opp period. And opps cry too.

***

"Symone, you're not going back there. We need to know how the fuck he knew you lived there. Luckily for you, the bullet went in and out," Cash said as he looked at her arm.

"I don't know. I just know he was in there waiting for me when I got home. I couldn't even pull my gun out on him. He had me down bad."

That's when Ray-J walked into the spot and looked at Symone and Cash.

"Ray-J, get some goons and go by Symone spot. Make sure her shit is locked up. She coming home with me tonight, and tomorrow we are going to clear it out."

"Kool. After I do that, I have a run to make, and I'll link up with y'all tomorrow to clear her shit out."

"That sound good to me."

Ray-J dapped Cash up and looked at Symone and said,

"Yo, cheer the fuck up. Niggas get shot every day. You going to live," he said with a smile on his face

"Fuck you Ray-J," Symone said as she laughed at him.

***

Gangstar rolled a blunt up as he thought about killing Cash. He promised himself that he would be dead in the streets before he would go back to prison. All his niggas are dead and the one motherfucker he would have gave his life up for was a fucking rat. His own personal homie from the sandbox he had to roll. He made his own bed, so he made sure he lay in it. With his face all over the news, there was only one female he trusted. Tasha respected his gangster, and she let him lay low at her spot. As he lit his blunt, Tasha came walking through the door with some fast food for the both of them.

"Gangstar, I got some food for us. You good?"

"I'm hungry as fuck. Good looking. That's mad love, baby girl."

"You know I got you playboy without no questions."

Gangstar got up, walked to Tasha and passed her the blunt as he grabbed a taco out of the bag.

"What's the word on the streets with Cash?"

"I ain't hear nothing. It's super-hot out there right now. After the police killing, everyone is staying off the blocks. The jump out boys are jumping out on everybody they see on the street."

"Cool. I'ma lay low still but I ain't going out bad. Cash is going to feel my fucking Gangstar. That's on the set.

Chapter 35

Animal was watching the news, shaking his head as he puffed on his blunt. He looked at Killer and said, "This shit is fucking crazy. All these fucking bodies dropping because you have two niggas trying to be the king on the fucking throne. Now, you got 5.0 jumping out on niggas flooding the block and fucking my money up."

"Real talk. That nigga Gangstar knew he wasn't ready to go toe to toe with Cash, not saying he ain't built like that. But them Brown Boys are real hittas and killers."

"Yeah, this nigga got Brooklyn hot while he hiding out in Stapleton Houses in Staten Island."

"How you know he's over there?"

"Killer, I don't give a fuck what the streets say. Remember, I really run New York and I know every fucking thing."

"I'm already knowing, Animal. Hands down."

Animal puffed on his blunt as he finish watching the news.

***

Cash walked around the room, looking at his workers break down the kilos of cocaine on the table. All the females had on was thongs with nothing else. Cash trusted nobody at all when it came down to his money. Big Apple walked in the spot and Cash walked up to him.

116

"What's the vibe, Apple?"

"Shit. just seeing if you are ready for a pickup. That's all."

"Yeah, I've got ten kilos ready for you now."

"Yeah, let me get that off your hands and drop that off to Rip."

"Let me go grab that. I'll be right back, homie."

Big Apple was looking at one of the females named Carma. She was light skin with a banging body. He'd been feeling her, but the rules was no fucking the workers. But in his mind, rules was meant to be broken. Cash walks out of the back room with a bookbag in his hand as he passed the bookbag to Big Apple.

"That shit is better than pussy, homie."

"My guy, anything that makes money is better than pussy, except pussy that is making money." Both of them dapped each other up and started laughing when Big Apple said that.

"Yo, I'm out, bro."

"Be smooth out there, Big Apple. You know the block is hot."

"I'm smoother than a baby ass. I got you, bro. Be safe."

"Copy that."

Big Apple walked out of the spot, knowing there was money to be made. In his eyes, fuck the police.

"Candy, how we looking over there?" Cash asked her.

"We are on the last one now, Cash. We should be done in about an hour or so."

Cash pulled the blunt and walked back off.

***

Tasha walked into Nicole's apartment, and called out her name. "Nicole, where the fuck you at bitch? We need to talk."

Nicole came walking out the back room with her robe on.

"Bitch, you know the door is there for a reason. Knock, wait, then when I open the door, you come in."

"Girl, please. What you got going on?"

"What you talking about?"

"Bitch don't act like you don't know what I'm talking about. What's this I hear you riding around with Style-B in the drop top Ferrari Spider. Yeah, a bitch heard you was with him over there in Castle Hill Houses in the Bronx, girl."

"Damn, you all up in my Kool-Aid, girl."

"What the fuck ever. Spill the beans. I want to know everything."

"Damn, okay. A bitch can't keep nothing to herself."

"Nope."

"Naw, Style-B is cool. I met him at Cloud 9 last week. I slid him my phone number and we been talking since. So, he asked me did I want to go out to eat yesterday. We went out had a few drinks and he brought me around some of his peoples in the Bronx. That's all."

"I heard he got a check."

"Yeah, he is caked up. I seen that for myself last night."

"So, you ain't fuck him last night?"

"No, I ain't fuck him. Every bitch is throwing pussy at him. I'm showing him I'm different."

"I hear you girl, and why ain't you dressed? What you about to do?"

"I'm about to take a shower and get ready to go to the club. You know that's how a bitch makes her money."

"I hear you, girl. Well I'm about to head back to the house. I'll call you tomorrow."

"Okay." Tasha got up and gave Nicole a hug before walking out of the door. Tasha was a bad bitch and she knew it. She would do whatever it took to get to the bag and that's why Gangstar respected her so much.

Chapter 36

Gangstar put on his black hoodie and black sweatpants with a pair of black Timberland boots. He grabbed his gun and walked out of the apartment. He got into his black Acura and pulled off headed to Brooklyn. He still had some business to take care of as far as he was concerned. Browns and everyone who was rocking a brown flag name was on that grocery list and he was going to eat his food. It took him 45 minutes to get to Brooklyn. He pulled up at Red Hook Projects, stepped out of his car and walked up to this dude named Black, who he knew was holding the Projects down.

"What's the word Black? How you living homie?"

Black looked at Gangstar and smiled. "What the fuck? I thought you would be MIA with your face all over the news."

"Nigga I ain't going no fucking where. Fuck the police, real talk. Next time they put they hands on me, I'll be getting placed in a body bag. On gang, homie."

"Nigga, I feel you on that shit. I ain't never going back up north again but what brings you way over here?"

"You already know how I feel about Cash. That nigga really got me down bad, so you know I'm after blood. I ain't going to rest until I kill that pussy ass nigga and anybody that fucks with him." Black puffed on his blunt before talking. "I know where one of his little homies be at all the time. Real talk."

"Who the fuck you talking about?"

"Ray-J."

"Where the fuck that nigga be at?"

"Castle Hill Houses in the Bronx, rolling dice and kicking the bobo over there."

"Word? That little nigga is about to be a dead motherfucker."

"Slow down, killer. He don't be by himself. You might want to get a bitch to get him because if you go over there you ain't got to worry about the police finding you because they are going to be called to pick your body up off the streets in a pool of blood."

"Say less, I got you. Good looking, homie."

"Already dog, be safe in these streets. Stay dangerous."

Gangstar smiled and lifted up his shirt, showing Black his Glock-9 on his waist. "I stay dangerous hands down"

***

Nicole came from the back locker room wearing a G-string and 6 inch high heels with nothing else on. The club was packed with people. The music was blasting. You had two girls on stage dancing. You had the guys throwing money on the stage. Nicole looked around and saw Style-B in the corner, smoking a blunt with a bottle in his hand. He was alone in the VIP just chilling. She walked over to him and sat on his lap.

"Why you ain't tell me you were coming out here tonight?"

"It was a last moment thing beautiful, but I see you in here looking sexy as fuck, baby girl."

"You know I got to get this money."

"I told you the other day you ain't got to do this. I got you."

"I know you got me but let me make this money, daddy and I'll take care of you later, Okay?"

"Okay sexy, I got you."

Tasha walked into the club and sat down at the bar. She saw Nicole in the corner talking to Style-B. Tasha was bad and the outfit she had on was hugging her hourglass body. She watched as Style-B got up and kissed Nicole as he was getting ready to leave the club. Tasha smiled and walked outside the club, waiting on Style-B. Style-B walked outside up to his Mercedes-Benz AMG SL Roadster. She walked up to him.

"Nice car. It fit you." Style-B looked at Tasha.

"Damn sexy, that outfit is fitting that body. What's your name, beautiful?"

"Tasha."

"You work up in here, Tasha?"

"Respectfully, no. I can't see myself shaking my ass for a few dollars. Worldstar will not have my ass on a pole going viral. Sorry, that's not for me."

"Yo, I respect that. So, how you get your money?"

"Let's just say, anything a nigga can do, I can do, if not better."

"I like your style. Look Tasha, they call me Style-B. How about we go get something to eat, on me?"

"That's cool, but let me ask. Do you have someone you talking to because I don't have time to be be fucking no bitch up over some dick that I ain't never have."

Style-B laughed. "Naw, lil mama. I ain't got no chick, I have a friend but that's all she is, is a friend. Real talk."

"I can go for that."

"So, we going out to eat?"

"Yeah, we are, Style-B."

Style-B nodded, walked around the car and opened the door for Tasha to get inside. She smiled, knowing she was about to get to his bag.

***

"Pay me my fucking money. 456 bitches," Ray-J said as he was talking shit at the dice game.

"Nigga run that shit back, double or nothing. Matter fact, I have five hundred saying you can't, nigga," Kodak said to him.

"Nigga five hundred? Fuck that shit put a rack down. What the fuck you talking about son?"

"Nigga bet. Run that shit, baby boy."

Ray-J smiled and rolled the dice against the wall and watched as they rolled to 456 again on the first roll.

"What the fuck you talking about? I do this shit for real nigga Browns. Pay me my fucking money, boy."

Ray-J was talking shit as he was counting up his money. Gangstar was looking at them in the cut as he smoked his blunt, watching Ray-J talk his shit. Black did put him on point. There wasn't no way he could rock Ray-J to sleep. They was too deep over there. Plus, he could tell they all was holding but he knew how to get him. He smiled and drove off.

***

"Damn daddy, this was what you meant when you said you wanted something to eat," Tasha said as Style-B had her legs up in the air licking and sucking all over her pussy. She had her hands on his head cumming all over his lips.

"Baby girl, I want you to come ride this dick for me."

"I got you, daddy." Tasha unbuttoned Style-B's pants and pulled his thick, long manhood out. She couldn't believe how big he was. She let out a loud moan as she slid down his dick and started riding him. She held onto the driver seat of the Benz.

"Damn baby, this pussy is wet as hell. This that water water."

Tasha leaned forward in the car as she was riding him and said in his ear, "You like this pussy, daddy?"

"Hell yeah."

Tasha started riding his dick faster and harder so she could feel Style-B's nut all inside of her. She stopped riding him and looked into his eyes.

"Damn you fucked me up with that good good, baby girl."

"The way you was putting that dick down. You was making this pussy curve to it."

"You are too much for TV, Tasha. So, what's up you chilling with me for the rest of the night?"

"I got you for a little while longer. Then, I have somethings I need to do."

"Cool, that works for me."

Tasha knew she was dead wrong, but if Nicole wasn't going to get to the bag, shit she was. All it took was a good fuck and she ain't even suck his dick. He already want her around him all night.

Chapter 37

Test pulled up to the spot with the two duffle bags in the trunk of the car. He waited until Rip turned the backlight on before he opened the car door and popped the trunk. He stepped out of the car, got the bags and walked into the spot. He dapped Rip up as he walked inside.

"How we looking out there, playboy?"

"It's hot as fuck. Them boys in blue in everywhere right now."

"I already know. How many you bring with you?"

"I got ten. Five in each bag. I thought Big Apple told you."

"That nigga might have but I got so much shit going on it might have slipped my mind."

"Just stay on point. You know Gangstar is still out there, and Cash wants that nigga rolled in the worst way."

"I already be knowing. If I see that boy, I'm putting every shell in his head that I have in this Glock-9."

"Nigga you ain't the only one. I see that nigga and I'm pushing his biscuit back, on gang gang."

"Facts. Look, let me start pushing this work out and I'll get at you later, bro."

"Already, fam." Test got into his car and looked around before pulling off, making sure the police wasn't on the block.

***

Tasha walked into the house and up to Gangstar as he was on the couch watching an old school Gangstar movie.

"What's up, Tasha? Where you been?"

"Just trying to put some shit together, that might be able to benefit us in the long run."

"What you got in mind?"

"Just a nigga who I know to get a few dollars; that's all."

"Just let me know. You know I'm down for the murder game anytime, but check me out. I need you to get close to a nigga and set him up for me."

"Who you talking about setting up? You know I got you."

"This little nigga Ray-J. He's one of Cash little homies."

"I got you. Where can I find him at?"

"I know he be at Castle Hill Houses in the Bronx."

"Don't even worry about it. We got this, the coldhearted way."

"That's why I put my fucking trust in you. Real talk."

Tasha just nodded and walked to the room to get ready for the shower.

***

Cash was smoking a cigar, listening to Symone as she talked.

"Cash, everyone been looking for Gangstar. He's nowhere to be found. He might not even be in the city no more."

"That nigga is in the city. He just ducked off right now. Put a brick on that nigga head. That's going to have the whole city looking for his ass. We can't have a nigga like that running around. A motherfucker like that need to be in a box."

"I'm on it. I'm going to put the word out."

"Symone, you know Gangstar better than any of us. Where would he go?"

"He wouldn't leave Brooklyn. He's somewhere in Brooklyn— Marry Houses, Brownsville, Red Hook, Van Dyke Houses— real talk. I don't know where he is at right now."

"I believe you. Just make sure you stay with that fire on you at all times."

"Always." Symone lifted up her shirt, showing off her baby 9 she had in the waistband of her pants.

Cash nodded at her as she walked off.

***

Style-B walked into his spot and took off all the jewelry. He took the bag he had in his hand and walked to the safe. He opened his safe up. There was $1.5-million he had in there. He placed the $50,000 he made for the week in the safe. Style-B was a smart hustler. He ain't post up on the block selling drugs or sit in a dope house. He learned the scamming game and ran his check up, but his business was his business and that's all that mattered.

He walked to his bed and laid down. It was 1AM. As soon as he closed his eyes the phone went off. He picked it up to see it was Nicole calling him. "What's up, beautiful?"

"Nothing, just getting off work. I wanted to know if you wanted to see me."

"I'm not going to lie to you. I'm just now getting in the bed. I been running all over the city. How about we link up tomorrow afternoon, sexy?"

"Okay. I'm with that, daddy."

"Cool. I'll see you tomorrow, baby girl."

"Okay."

Style-B hung up and closed his eyes, thinking about Tasha.

Chapter 38

Gangstar pulled up to one of Cash's old traps. He just wanted to see if he was still moving weight out of there. He'd been posted up for the last hour in the cut. He saw a few people going in and out of there. It'd been quiet for the last 20 minutes. Gangstar put his hoodie on and cocked back his gun. He looked both ways before stepping out of the car and ran across the street. He kicked the door opened. As soon as he stepped in the trap, he shot the two dudes on the couch and pointed the gun at the other dude. He looked at his two homies on the couch.

"It's no point to look at them. Them motherfuckers are dead. You know what the fuck I'm here for. I want the bag and the work now, nigga. Test my fucking Gangstar."

"Chill, chill. I got the money and the work in the back."

"So take me to it, motherfucker." Gangstar walked him to the back room, gun pressed to the back of his head.

"Everything is right there. It's two kilos and about $20,000 in the bag."

"That's what the fuck I'm talking about. Good looking, nigga." Gangstar pulled the trigger, blowing his brains out. He watched as his body hit the floor. He picked up the bag with the money and work and ran out of the house to his car and pulled off, leaving three dead bodies in Cash's trap.

***

The Cadillac Escalade Platinum Edition pulled up on the block. Cash rolled the back window down and was watching the scene with all the police everywhere as CSI was all in his trap. He rolled the window up and looked at Big Apple. "You and I both know this has Gangstar's name written all over it."

"How much work was in the house?"

"A little over two birds. We have to get this nigga fast. I want to stand over his lifeless body bad as fuck."

"That nigga day is coming, Cash. He can't run forever. You get us out of here."

"Yes, sir."

"Apple. I put a kilo on this nigga head."

"You should have put two. Real talk."

"Say less then." Cash puffed on his cigar as they drove off.

***

Tasha walked into the apartment and saw Gangstar bagging up dope and smoking a blunt. She walked up to the table and picked up one of the kilos. "Damn, what's all this?"

"I caught 3 of Cash niggas slipping so I ran down on them, hard. I bodied they ass and took the work and bread out they spot. Facts."

"How much cash you get them for?"

"$20,000. I put $10,000 in your room on the dresser. You know, for holding me down."

"Yo, that's real good looking, Gangstar. A bitch needed that."

"You already know I got your back; hands down. And this is just the start. Wait 'til I get a new team. I'm taking shit back over."

"You looking for some niggas? I know a few shooters."

"Not right now. I'm still blazing hot, but I am going to need someone to help me get this work off."

"I may know someone if you want me to pull up on them."

"Yeah, do that, but keep my name out of it. I don't need nobody to know me and you are linked up. They might want to drop a dime to the police and get that bag that's on my head."

"I got you, Gangstar."

"Already." Gangstar handed Tasha the bookbag with a half of a kilo inside. "That's half of a brick. I need 25 racks for that."

"Cool. I got this." Tasha took the bag and walked back out the spot.

***

Cash looked around at everybody in the room before talking. "I been hustling. I been stepping like the mob. My body count is real. I don't be telling y'all what to do because I think I know it all. I really be trying to get y'all to move like me. Look what just happened to the three homies. All them niggas rolled and all the work and money is gone. Hands down, I know it was Gangstar, but don't nobody know where the fuck this nigga is. What I do know is that he is watching us to know what spots to hit of ours. Real talk. This nigga ain't playing. He's pulling that trigger."

Cash looked at Big Apple and nodded.

"If y'all niggas got a death wish, take your tool and put it in your mouth and take your life. So, this fuck nigga got two birds. It's no point to asking question because he can get them off in any of the five— Boroughs, Brooklyn, Queens, the Bronx, Manhattan, or Staten Island. We just need y'all to be on point. That's all we saying, so y'all won't end up in a black bag."

"Look, respectfully, this nigga has nothing to lose, so he is taking gambles with his life. We just can't put our lives on pause because this nigga in the streets with a gun," Amen said.

"We ain't saying put your life on pause; we are saying move smart or you might be the next nigga to take a dirt nap. That's all," Cash said

"This is how we are moving from now on. Test is doing all pick-ups, everyone else hold your spot down. Everybody understand?"

Everyone nodded at Cash. He looked at everyone and walked off.

Chapter 39

"Damn, sexy, what's good? You are looking too good right now."

Nicole smiled as she got into Style-B's car. "Whatever, nigga," Nicole said, playing as she reached over and kissed Style-B.

"So, where you trying to go out to eat at, beautiful?"

"There is this spot in Queens I want to go check out."

"That's where we going then, sexy." Style-B pulled off, playing Cardi-B.

Nicole looked at him and smiled. She pushed her seat back, leaned over and unbuttoned his pants, pulling his thick manhood out.

He looked down at her. "That's what we doing, sexy?"

"Yeah. Just drive, daddy. I got this down here."

Style-B laughed as Nicole started sucking on his manhood, licking all around the head. She was licking up and down the neck of his manhood before she started deep throating him.

Style-B put his hand on her head. "Damn, baby, this shit feel good as fuck. You got a nigga ready to bust all in your mouth. Fuck, bae."

"Go ahead, daddy, and I'm drink everything that comes out of this dick."

Style-B pulled over as he started fucking Nicole all in her mouth. Nicole was sucking his dick so good that when he started to nut, he moaned out her name. "Nicole, fuck."

Nicole sucked all his nut up and patted him on the leg to show him his nut all over her tongue before she closed her mouth and swallowed it.

"Damn, I needed that, baby."

"I know you did, daddy." Nicole fixed her seat back as Style-B drove off.

***

Savage watched as Tasha's car pulled up on the block.

Tasha stepped out the car looking fly as hell as she walked up to Savage.

"What's rocking, fam? What brings you up over here, looking like a runway model?"

"I thought you might be trying to get some money."

"Real talk, what you got in mind?"

"Walk with me to my car real quick. Let me show you something."

Savage walked to Tasha's car, got inside, and closed the door.

"Look, I got this half of a bird I'm trying to get 25K for. You know anybody who might want to cop it?"

"Damn, this that pure white girl, too. I can just look at it. Where you get this shit from, fam?"

"You know I got my people I deal with, but you know someone, fam?"

"Yeah, I do. Let me make a call real quick. Hold up." Savage pulled out his phone and called Wolf.

After a few rings, Wolf picked up the phone. "What's up, little homie? What's the business?"

"I got this half of a bird for 25K. You fucking with it?"

"You talking sideways over the phone. Pull up at my spot, homie."

"Say less. I'm on my way now, fam."

Wolf hung up the phone and puffed on his blunt.

"Savage, this nigga ain't on no funny shit is he?"

132

"Nah, I don't think so, but you never know out here in these streets."

"I dealt with him before on some shit, but I stay holding just in case." Tasha shook her head and opened the glove box, pulling out her baby 9-millimeter.

"Damn, fam, you holding heat and the work. You out here on the block for real, huh?"

"I'm just doing what I need to do, that's all. Where we headed, Savage?"

"We going to Van Dyke Houses."

Tasha put her sunglasses on and pulled off.

***

Tasha walked into the project with Savage up to Wolf's door. She had the bookbag on her back. Savage knocked twice before Wolf opened the door for them to walk inside.

Savage dapped Wolf up as he walked into the apartment. "What's the word, Wolf? How you, fam?"

"I'm good, homie. Who is this you got with you?"

"This is my fam Tasha. She the one who got that half of bird for the 25K."

"What's up, Tasha? Let me see what you working with, ma."

Tasha took the bookbag off and passed it to Wolf.

He placed it on the table and opened it up

"Yeah, this that white bitch. Okay, lil' mama, I'll give you $15,000 right now for it."

"We must have a communication problem because Savage just told you 25K."

"Look, I just told you 15K. You want it or you don't?"

"Naw, I'm good, homie. Let me get that bag back,"

"So, y'all going to pull up at my spot and waste my fucking time?"

"Hol' up, nigga. We told you 25K from the jump. You tripping," Savage said.

That's when Wolf pulled out his Glock .40 and pointed it at them. "Now this is my shit. Get the fuck up out my spot, pussy ass niggas."

Tasha closed her eyes then turned around. She pulled her gun out. Wolf was so focused on Savage that he didn't see Tasha. She turned around fast and started shooting at Wolf. He ducked. Savage pulled his gun out and shot Wolf in the chest, killing him. He then patted him down as Tasha grabbed the bookbag.

"Savage, we need to get the fuck out of here, now!"

"Man, fuck that. Where this nigga money at? I know he is holding."

Tasha looked to the left and saw a shoe box on the floor. She opened it up and saw stacks of $100 bills. "I got the money! Come on! We have to go, now!"

They walked out of Wolf's spot, got into Tasha's car and pulled off leaving, Wolf dead in a pool of blood with tears in his eyes.

***

Symone walked up to Black in Red Hook Projects.

He was sitting on the bench, smoking a blunt, but got up when he saw her. "Little Gangstar Symone. What the fuck is rocking?"

"I'm out here living, Black. What's the word?"

"You see what I'm doing. I'm out here smoking, getting to the bag, baby girl. You know that nigga Gangstar was around here two days ago."

"What that nigga was talking about?"

Black pulled on the blunt one more time then passed it to Symone. "Getting at Cash and his people, still. You know that nigga ain't letting shit go. Facts."

"You ain't hear what happened, Black, with me, Gangstar and Showtime?"

"Hell to da no. What went down, Little Gangstar?"

"A little over a year ago, they had me set up one of Cash little homies. Shit went sideways and them niggas got me down bad. Tied me up and put the pump to my head."

"Fuck no. I ain't hear no shit like that. That's on gang, Symone."

"It get deeper than that, fam." Symone puffed the blunt and passed it back.

"So tell me what the fuck happened."

"Cash and Big Apple called them clown ass niggas and told them they was going to flatline me and all. On speaker I heard every word. Them niggas said, 'Fuck that bitch, nigga. Body her,' then they hung up the phone."

"So how the fuck you get up out of there?"

"Cash asked me where Gangstar lived. I looked at him and rolled my eyes. Big Apple was going to kill me, but Cash saw I was a loyal bitch and gave me a pass after I tried to set one of his hittas up."

"That was real. If that nigga ain't have a heart, he would have flatlined your ass."

"Real talk. That nigga showed me mad love after that shit went down with Gangstar."

"What you mean?"

"Real talk, no cut, I started running with Cash. He put me in a fly ass spot and made my pockets deep. He showed me more loyalty and love than Gangstar ever did."

"So you Brown's now, Symone?"

Symone pulled up her shirt sleeve and showed Black her tattoo that said *Browns* in big letters.

"Damn, Gangstar ain't try and clap you about the shit?"

"Money and Killer-B tried to run up on me, but I pulled out and blasted Killer-B, and shot it out with Money."

"So you the one who killed Killer-B?"

"He ran up and I pulled out first. It was either him or me."

"You need to watch your back. He's out here looking for blood; hands down. Matter of fact, he said something about he know that one of Cash homies be in Castle Hill Houses in the Bronx when he was here. Real talk."

"Good looking, Black, on that info. Real talk."

"Always, Symone. Stay up."

"You, too." Symone turned around and walked off as she pulled her phone out to call Cash.

***

"I can't believe shit just popped off like that. I thought you knew that nigga, Savage."

"Yo, fuck that nigga. He's dead now. Ain't shit we can do about it. You got the work and the bag so that's all a win-win, hands down."

"How much is in that box?"

Savage opened the shoe box and looked inside. "It have to be close to $200,000, fam. All theses 100s."

Tasha took the shoe box from Savage, pulled out two stacks of $100 bills and passed them to Savage. "I know that's over $50,000, and this half of brick is yours, fam."

"Good looking, cuz. Real talk."

"You know how we get down already."

"Facts." Savage got out of Tasha's car with the bookbag as he walked into his spot.

Tasha looked back in the shoe box where there were 8 more stacks of $100 bills. She knew there was close to $400,000 left in that box. Savage was her little cuz but she did right by him and Gangstar, so she had her ice-cream and cake, too.

Chapter 40

"Nicole, when you going to stop working at that club? I told you I got you, sexy."

Nicole shook her head. "Style-B, look. That's how I get my money. I don't ask you how you get yours, now do I?"

"I'm just saying, I don't want my shorty shaking her ass no more. Real talk. We are up-up right now."

"No, you are up right now, not me."

"That's how you feel?"

"Style, I sucked your dick for the first time today. We only been talking for two weeks. You ain't stamped nothing yet."

"So let's stamp this shit then. From here on out, you are my shorty; hands down."

Nicole started smiling. "Now, you got some say so in my life."

"What the fuck ever, Nicole."

Nicole got up and sat next to Style-B in the restaurant. "We going to do this together, baby?"

"Yeah, Nicole, we are going to do this together."

***

Tasha walked up to Gangstar and threw him the 25K with a smile on her face. Gangstar smiled back at her as he counted the money.

"Damn, I see you are really in these streets, Tasha."

"I just know a few people, that's all, Gangstar. But you know I got you."

Gangstar stood up so he was face to face with Tasha. He ain't say nothing to her; he just grabbed her by the waist, pulled her closer to him and started kissing her like she was the last female on earth. Tasha closed her eyes and started kissing him back. Gangstar picked Tasha up and carried her to the bedroom. He laid her down on the bed as he pulled his shirt off, showing her his tattoo-coveres chest and abs. Tasha never took her eyes off of him as he started to pull his pants down along with his boxers, showing off his thick manhood. Tasha licked her lips as she started to take her clothes off, showing her hourglass body. She laid back on the bed and opened her legs, showing off her clean, shaved pussy. Gangstar grabbed her legs and placed them on his shoulders as he placed his manhood inside her. Tasha let out a light moan.

"Damn, you wet as fuck, baby, and tight as hell."

"No, you just a big dick nigga. Damn."

Gangstar started fucking Tasha with long, deep strokes as she dug her nails into his back. She started to bite his neck as he was fucking her.

"Gangstar, I'm about to cum. Damn, daddy, I'm about to come all over this dick."

"Go ahead, because this is my pussy, now. On gang." Gangstar held Tasha tight as he started to cum deep inside of her.

Tasha came all over Gangstar's dick as she looked into his eyes.

***

"Yo, Cash, I just left Red Hook Projects."

Cash nodded at Symone. "Word? And what's over there?"

"Black. He one of the hustlers over there. He said that Gangstar was just over there a few days ago and that he know you have a little homie that be in Castle Hills Houses in the Bronx."

"He's talking about Ray-J. He be over there rolling dice, kicking shit with them niggas over there."

"You want me to call Ray-J and let him know?"

"No, I'm going to call Ray-J. What I need you to do is to find out where this nigga is laying his fucking head down at."

"I been going to all the old spots. That nigga is MIA. Real talk."

"Yo, just keep looking for me, Symone."

"Say less. I'm on the block."

"Stay safe out there."

"Always, big bro."

Cash pulled out his phone and called Ray-J.

After a few seconds, Ray-J picked up. "Cash, what's the business?"

"Gangstar knows you be at Castle Hill Houses, so you need to be on point."

"Already. If I see that nigga, I'ma roll his ass, on Browns."

"Say less. I'm just putting you on point."

"That's love. big bro."

"Facts. You got my number if you need me."

"Already." Ray-J hung up and looked around before going back to the dice game.

***

"Tasha, look. You are my down as bitch; hands down. You showed me you are more loyal than these niggas in the street, and I respect your Gangstar, baby, but I need you to do something for me, love."

Tasha laid her head on Gangstar's chest as she listened to him. "What you need me to do, Gangstar. I got you."

"I need you to post up over at Castle Hill Houses. There's this nigga name Ray-J over there. He's one of Cash peoples. I got that nigga name on the grocery list. I need to add him to my graveyard."

"I got you, daddy. I'll post up there tomorrow and see what he's talking about."

"Good looking, baby girl."

"But there is something I need from you."

"And what's that, sexy?"

"You have to help me with my needs."

"You don't never have to worry about that. I got you, long-dick-style." Gangstar kissed her forehead as he laid in the bed with Tasha in his arms.

Chapter 41

"Son, I see you got the block on smash, homie," Jamaica said to Savage.

"Naw, fam, I'm just trying to eat with the little crumbs that I have. That's all." Savage passed the blunt he was smoking to Jamaica.

"You heard that nigga Wolf got popped last week?"

"Hell to da no. By who? Did they say, Jamaica?"

"That's the word that's floating in the air, bro," Jamaica said as he puffed on the blunt.

"Nigga, you ain't say if they know who did it or not."

"They don't know who rolled his ass. They just know son got bodied. That's all."

"You already know how them niggas get down over there at them Van Dyke Houses. Facts."

"Big facts. But fuck all that. Weren't you over there at them Van Dyke Houses?"

"Look, you my brother; hands down; so you know I'm only eating if you are eating with me." Savage reached into his pocket and pulled out two ounces of cocaine and passed it to Jamaica

"Damn, this is how you are living, dawg?"

"Naw, that's how we are living. That's you, family, on the love tip."

"Already. From the steps to the block, I got you, homie."

"I already know. Now pass my blunt nigga" both of them started laughing. Savage was only 16 but he had the heart of a lion and so did Jamaica that's why they were so close.

***

Tasha sat in her car watching Ray-J as he was talking to a few dudes on the block. She couldn't lie, Ray-J was slick fly and he knew how to dress, but most of all he was about his money and she could tell. She stepped out of her car and walked over to him. She was looking like a real boss bitch and she knew it.

Ray-J looked at her and walked over to her with a smile on his face. "Damn, sexy, where the fuck you come from?"

"I'm from Brooklyn. Brownsville. What about you?"

"I lived in all the Projects. So what's your name?"

"Tasha. So are we about to play 21 questions? If so, what's your name?"

"Ray-J, little mama. Come on a walk with me to the bench so we can talk one-on-one."

Tasha smiled as she walked off with him, knowing he was just a weak link that she was just going to toy with; nothing more. As she went to sit down, she got a text message from Style. *"I'm trying to see you tonight if you ain't busy."*

She replied, *"I'll call you in a hour."*

"So, what brings you around, beautiful?"

Tasha smiled as she looked at Ray-J. "I just felt like riding around. That's all."

Ray-J nodded. "Well, I'm glad that you did."

***

Cash pulled up to the front of the Projects. he looked around before going and knocking on B-God's baby mother's apartment door. Her name was Monica. It'd been 6 months since B-God was dead. After a few minutes the door opened and Cash was looking dead at Monica and her daughter, Adrian, as Monica was holding her in her arms

"What's up, Monica? How are you holding up?"

"I'm living, Cash. Come inside." Monica moved out the way for Cash to walk into the apartment.

"Monica, again, I'm sorry for how shit played out with B-God. Just know I'm here for you and baby girl, always."

"Thank you, Cash. That really means a lot to me. But B-God knew what came with the life he lived; he always said it was a matter of time before he got caught down bad."

"Yeah, he used to say that a lot to me, too. Look I'm not going to stay long. I just came to check on you and baby girl and to drop this off to you, Monica." Cash reached into his pocket, pulled out two knots of $100 bills, and passed it to Monica. "Look, that's $100,000; $50,000 in each knot. I know that can't bring back B-God but it's the least that I can do for you."

Monica had tears in her eyes. "Thank you so much, Cash. Thank you." Monica placed Adrian down on the couch as she got up and hugged Cash.

Cash kissed her on the forehead. "Look, you know how to reach me if you need anything."

"I do."

Cash looked at Adrian one more time before walking out the apartment. Monica was beautiful. She was bad, she was loyal, and that's what Cash respected about her the most. He made a promise to B-God that he would forever hold her down for him no matter what.

***

Tasha walked up to the park where Style-B was sitting on the hood of his car, smoking a blunt, looking at Tasha's sexy ass as she walked up to him.

"What's up, player?"

"Shit, thinking about you. You got me licking my lips like I'm on my way to Candy Land."

"You could be. You know I do taste like candy; I was told."

"Yes, you do, beautiful."

Tasha looked around. "Who you know over here in Shuy Town?"

"Shit. nobody really. I live over here."

"Okay, baller, I see you."

"Come on. Let me show you my spot and how I'm living."

"Okay, let me see how you are living, pimping."

Style-B walked Tasha into his spot. She couldn't believe how fly his spot was. He had a chandelier dangling above the custom sofa. His centerpieces was fly as hell. Even the ceiling beams. The kitchen countertops were made in Germany. He had two 72-inch TVs on the wall with a bear skin rug in front of the fireplace.

"Damn, you living, I see."

"A little something-something."

Tasha sat on the sofa as her phone was going off. She saw that it was Nicole calling her. "Who is that calling me?"

"So, pick up the phone for her, then."

Tasha smiled and picked up the phone. "Hey, girl, what's up?"

As soon as she picked up the phone, Style-B walked over to her and kneeled between her legs as he started to unbutton Tasha's pants, pulling them off along with her thongs as she slipped her shoes off with her legs opened up on the sofa. Style-B was licking all over her clit.

"Girl, let me tell you. Last night, Style-B took me out to eat in Quenn and asked me to be his girl."

Tasha was face fucking Style-B, rubbing her pussy all over his face and tongue as Nicole was talking to her. "Damn, that's your nigga, now?" Tasha said as she had her hand on Style-B's head.

"Yeah, girl, that's my boo thang, now."

"That's what's up, girl, but listen, let me call you back."

"Okay, I'm about to call him now. I'll talk to you later."

"Okay." Tasha hung up.

Not even 30 seconds went by and Style-B's phone was ringing. Tasha knew that it was Nicole calling him. She pushed Style-B on the floor, on his back so that she could sit on his face, putting her pussy all over his lips. She looked at his phone and saw it was Nicole calling him.

Style-B had his hands on her hips.

"Damn, baby, I'm about to nut all over your fucking tongue." Tasha started riding Style-B's face harder and harder. She picked up her phone and put the camera on as she started cuming. She squirted as much as she could all over his face as she squatted over him. Style-B had his eyes closed. She made sure she took two pictures of his face and her juices all over it without him knowing it. She then sat back on his face and rode him a little bit more before getting up.

"Damn, girl, was you trying to drown me?"

"Yep."

"I see." Style-B sat up and saw he had a missed call from Nicole. He stood up and looked at Tasha. "Yo, I'll be right back, sexy."

"Okay, daddy." Tasha smiled as he walked off.

***

Big Apple was smoking a blunt at Stapleton Houses in Staten Island as he waited for his homie Rip to make a play when he thought he saw Gangstar walking into the apartment building with a black hoodie on. He grabbed his gun and stepped out of the black Jeep Wrangler and walked towards the building. He stopped and called Gangstar's name as he was going up the steps. "Yo, Gangstar!"

Gangstar stopped walking and grabbed his gun. When he turned around, Big Apple started shooting at him. As he started shooting back at Big Apple, bullets was flying everywhere. Big Apple ducked to the side as Gangstar took off running up the stairs. Rip came running into the building, looking at Big Apple.

"Come on! Gangstar just ran up the stairs! I think I shot his ass."

They took off running up the stairs but Gangstar was gone.

"Fuck! Come on. Let's get the fuck out of here before them boys in blue come. But now we know where this nigga lay his head at now."

Gangstar was in Tasha's apartment. He knew he had to get out of there. It was too hot for him to stay there. He put all his money and drugs into a bookbag and walked out the spot to his car. As he was pulling off he saw the police coming his way.

Chapter 42

"Cash, I had the motherfucker right at the tips of my hand. As soon as I called his name he turned around and I started clapping at his ass. I know I hit that pussy ass nigga."

"And you said he was at Stapleton Houses?"

"Yeah. That bitch ass nigga was over there."

Cash nodded. "So now we know where this bitch nigga been hiding at."

Big Apple lit his blunt before talking. "I'm sending Amen and Soulja over there to see what they can find out. I need to know who spot he is posted up at."

"Yeah, that's smart. And tell them to be low key because 9 out of 10 times, it's a bitch house he was laid up in."

"Copy that. I'm about to get on that right now."

"Hit me when you know something, Apple."

"Say less."

Cash wanted Gangstar dead in the worst way. He hated everything about him, and he swore on Browns he was going to make sure that bitch-made gets rolled for trying Browns.

***

Tasha pulled up to her spot and police were everywhere. She stepped out of her car and walked past them on the way into her apartment. Once she got into her place, she noticed Gangstar was gone. She pulled out her phone and saw she had 6 missed calls from him. She called him right back within a few seconds.

He answered the phone. "Yo, Tasha where you been? I been blowing your phone up"

"I was doing what you asked me to do with Ray-J. What the fuck happened over here?"

"Shit went sideways. I don't know how niggas knew I was over there. I just heard someone call my name then bullets started blasting. Shit was bananas."

"Yeah, it's flooded with police over here right now. Where you at right now?"

"I'm over here at Edenwald Houses in the Bronx."

"Cool. I'm on my way to you now. Just stay put."

"Trust me, I'm not going nowhere."

Tasha hung up the phone and went inside her room. She moved her top mattress and pulled all her money out and counted it. She had $380,000. She put all her money in her bag and left. Just in case the police find out Gangstar was there and they decide to kick her door in, they wouldn't get her money. She got back into her car and drove off. She knew she was going to have to get another spot now. Not just because of the police, but because of Cash. Because he was sending his shooters, and bullets didn't have any names.

***

Jamaica walked up on Savage with his hoodie on, holding his gun under his shirt as he was looking over his shoulder.

"Son, what the fuck you walking up on me, holding your piece, looking like that for?"

"Bam just told me you got a ticket on your head. Word on the block: you and some bitch bodied Wolf and got off with a half a bag."

"Bam could suck my dick. I ain't pop that nigga."

"Bro. they said they got you on tape in that nigga spot. You and shorty walking into his spot before he was rolled, and y'all coming out of his shit holding a shoe box and a bookbag."

"Fuck-fuck!"

"Nigga, is there something you want to tell me?"

Savage shook his head. "Last week I called this nigga Wolf and told him I had a half a brick for 25K. He told me to pull up. I pulled up and the nigga started talking sideways out his mouth and tried to lick me, so I upped the fire and flatlined his ass."

"Look, you know I'ma ride with you, hands down. Just know them Castle Hill niggas got your name on they hit list. Facts."

"Man, fuck them niggas. If they want smoke, I'm all for the fuck shit."

Before Savage could finish talking, two vans pulled up on him and four niggas jumped out holding NP-90s in their hands. Savage just shook his head as Killer walked up to him.

"Somebody wants to talk to you, little nigga, or I can just body your little ass right now. You and your man. What's it going to be?"

Savage nodded at Killer as Killer's men walked up to them and took their guns as they pushed them into the van. Killer got into the van and pulled off. Savage looked at Jamaica, not saying a word with a fucked up feeling going through his body.

***

"Gangstar, you good?"

"Yeah, I'm 100. It was just crazy as fuck how they had me down bad. Look, I need another spot to lay low at."

"I got that covered already. I got a motel for us to stay at tonight and tomorrow we are going to Queens. I have a friend who got a spot we can rent out."

"That's why I fuck with you. You always coming through at crunch time; hands down."

"I told you I got your back. You ride for me. I'm going to ride for you to the very end."

"That's why you are my Gangstar boo. Come on, let's get the fuck up out of here. I'm trying to get off these streets it's. Hot as fuck out here right now." Gangstar leaned all the way back in his seat as Tasha pulled off.

***

Savage walked into the Van Dyke Houses along with Jamaica and 6 niggas with guns behind them. Killer opened the apartment door. As they walked inside, Animal walked up to them, smoking a cigar.

"So, this the little nigga that killed Wolf and stole my money. And who the fuck is this nigga with him? His right hand man?"

"Yeah, I got both these little niggas together, posted on the block."

Animal puffed on his cigar before talking. "What's your name, nigga?"

"Savage."

"So you thought it was smart to kill one of my workers and steal my shit?"

"It ain't even go down like that. I pulled up seeing if he wanted to by a half a brick for 25K. He had me come to his spot and he got on the goofy shit with me, pulling his hammer out on me. That's when shit got bananas real fast."

"Who's this bitch you with?"

"She nobody."

"Who the fuck is she, though?"

Savage looked at the guns that Animal's homies had in their hands before talking. "Like I said, she nobody."

Killer put the gun to Savage's head. Savage just closed his eyes.

"Chill, Killer. This nigga is loyal to the bitch. I respect that, but this is what we going to do. This nigga Wolf had $400,000 of my money. That's gone now. So how we are going to make this right, I want my $400,000 back plus $200,000 for Wolf's body. And this is where shit get sweet. I want $400,000 just for having enough heart to pull that shit off, or I can just kill this nigga you with and we can just call it even."

Killer put the gun to Jamaica's head.

Savage looked at him then Animal. "You asking me to get you a meal ticket?"

"When you want to play gangster in these streets, know who the fuck you are dealing with. And there's more, nigga. Have my cake in 72 hours. This nigga is staying with me 'til you come back with my cake. If I don't hear from you in 72 hours with my bread, this nigga body will be floating in the East River where yours will be soon after."

"Yo, Jamaica, I got you, bro."

"I'm glad we got that cleared up. Killer, drop this nigga back off on the block. Let's see if he's really a fucking savage."

Savage looked at Jamaica and nodded as he walked out the apartment doors.

Chapter 43

Tasha looked at her phone as it was going off and saw that it was Savage blowing her up. She walked out the room and picked up the call. "Savage, what's up?"

"Shit just got real. This nigga Wolf peoples kidnapped me with my nigga Jamaica and put the NP90 to my face."

"What the fuck? What happened? How you get away?"

"He let me go and kept Jamaica and said I have 72 hours to get him a million fucking dollars or he's going to kill Jamaica, then come kill me next."

"Do he know about me?"

"Yeah, but I ain't give him your name."

"Look, where are you? I'm about to come get you now."

"I'm over here in Brownsville Houses."

"Stay there. I'm on my way to come get you."

"Cool."

Tasha hung up and left the apartment. It took her 45 minutes to reach Savage. When she pulled up, he was smoking a blunt. He looked at her and got into the car.

"Look, fam shit is crazy right now. Where the fuck we going to get a million dollars from?"

"Look, I may know where we can get it from but we are going to have to kill this nigga afterwards."

"I don't give a fuck. Let's do it."

"Okay. Just be on standby when I call your phone."

"Fam, we need to do this shit tonight."

"I know. Let me just get everything set up, okay?"

"Say less. I'm waiting on your call." Savage got out of the car and watched as Tasha pulled off.

Tasha called Nicole to see what she was doing.

After a few seconds, Nicole picked up. "Hey, girl. What you got going on?"

"Nothing. Just chilling with my boo, watching Tubi at his spot."

"Okay, I see you, beautiful."

"I have to go. I'll call you tomorrow when I get home, girl."

"Okay, sexy." Tasha hung up the phone and looked at the picture she took of Style-B when she was riding his face. She was going to use the picture when Nicole was feeling herself too much but she needed for them to have a fallout so she wouldn't be there when Savage kicked in his door. She used her TextNow number and sent the picture to Style-B's phone with a text that said, *"I had so much fun last night with you. Hope this picture makes you smile."*

Style-B looked at the picture, so did Nicole, and she read the message.

"What the fuck is this, Style-B? You already fucking on me?"

"Nicole, hold on. You are doing too much right now. Just chill."

"No. Fuck you, Style-B. Nigga, you ain't shit."

"Coming from the bitch who be shaking her ass in niggas' faces every night."

"You know what? You are fucking clown! Just take me home." Nicole walked out of Style-B's spot to his car.

Style-B walked out behind her.

Tasha watched as he got into the car with Nicole and pulled off. She pulled out her phone and called Savage.

After a few rings he picked up the phone. "Yeah, what's the word, fam?"

"How long will it take you to get to Stuy Town in Manhattan?"

153

"Shit, I can be there in, like, 25 minutes."

"Okay, you need to get here, now."

"I'm on my way."

Tasha hung up the phone. She didn't know how much money Style-B had but for her family's life, she needed it all. He fucked up anyway by taking her to his spot. Now he was a lick in her eyes.

***

Cash sat at the table talking with Symone as he smoked his cigar. "Symone, nobody is meant to last in this life we live. It's going to end two ways. Death or prison. History showed us that a 1000 times over, so I try to move different from the rest of these niggas in the streets."

"So, if you know that there's only two ways this life ends, why don't you get out while you are ahead?"

"Too many people die behind my Brown flag for me to just walk away. That will be some fake ass shit. So I have to ride this train to the last stop."

"You know, when you stopped Big Apple from killing me, that showed me you really wasn't cold-hearted. That's why I go so hard for you and the family. You showed me more love than Gangstar ever did."

Cash placed his cigar in the ashtray and looked at Symone. "You know, Gangstar lost everything over a half of a brick of coke. If the table was turned, I would have had a meeting with him and given him two bricks or a brick and $50,000 for the loss of his shooter and what my guy took from him. Being a boss is about making the right choices for you and your team. I had more numbers and more blocks, which means I had more shooters. He crashed everyone out, now he is on the run. Symone, you are going to make a choice, and that choice is you going to kill Gangstar or you're going to let him kill you. The day that you get him down bad, don't do no talking, just take care of the business."

"I know what I'm going to do. I'm going to body his ass."

"Good because with him alive, he is a threat to all of us."

"I promise you the first chance I get I'm going to kill his ass."

Cash just nodded as he picked up his cigar and relit it.

***

Savage sat on the steps as he waited for Style-B to pull up. He had his head down with a hoodie on. Tasha went over the plan and her part she was going to play. Savage saw when Style-B pulled up. He stepped out of his car, and was walking up the steps to his apartment. He walked past Savage in a state of rage. Savage stood up and ran behind Style-B as he was opening the apartment door. Savage smacked him in the back of the head.

As he hit the ground, Savage pointed his Glock .40 at his head. "Nigga, you know what the fuck this is."

Style-B just lowered his head, mad as hell he got caught slipping. "Yo, I don't have no money in here; just what I got on me. You can have that. Just don't kill me."

Savage shot him in the knee cap.

Style-B let out a loud yell as he rolled over on the floor.

"Now, let's try this shit again, nigga."

"Yo, the safe is in the room! You can have all that shit! Just don't kill me!"

"So? You better hop your ass in there and open it before you bleed the fuck out and this bitch!"

Style-B held on to the walls as he made his way to the back room. He moved the painting on the wall and opened the safe for Savage before he fell back down on the floor.

Savage pulled a bag out and took everything in the safe he had in there. He looked down at Style-B and pointed the gun at his head. "I should kill you, but real talk, I'm let you live."

Style-B didn't say anything. As Savage turned around, Style-B pulled his gun out. As he was pointing it at Savage, Tasha came from the other room and shot Style-B in the chest, killing him. Savage turned around and saw the gun in Style-B's hand, then looked back at Tasha, holding her gun

"I'm glad you ain't locked the door. Come on. We have to go now."

When they made it out of Style-B's spot, Tasha took Savage back to her apartment where they went inside and counted up the money.

"Savage, I told you to kill that nigga."

"Look, there's something I need to tell you."

"Word? What's that?"

"I been running with Gangstar for the last few months."

"That's where you got that work from. I been trying to get down with him. That's been the big homie from day one."

"Look, he's hot right now, but when the time is right, I'll put you on to him. Right now, let's take care of this business."

"Word. We have $1.3 million right plus mad jewels."

"Look, split the $300,000 between us so we can go take care of this other dude. Who is he by the way?"

"Real talk, the only name I remember was Killer."

"You ready to go handle this business?"

"Tasha, they don't know who you are and I want to keep it that way."

"They don't got to see my face, but I am taking you over there."

"Cool, let's ride out."

Chapter 44

Animal smoked his cigar as he walked around his apartment. He looked at his watch. It was 10PM he walked up to Jamaica who was sitting at the table. "You little niggas got heart. If you wasn't so young, I would have put you two niggas in a graveyard for stealing my shit."

"Savage told you your dude wasn't living right. He upped the fire first and he got bodied behind that."

"That could have been the way shit went down, but I don't fucking know that. All I know is that one of my workers is dead and my money is gone. So that put y'all niggas in the hot seat."

"My round ain't even 17 years old yet and you got him out there trying to come up with a meal ticket in the heart of the city."

"It's not about the mil; it's about to see if he's going to come back for you or not. I want to see where that nigga loyalty is, plus I want my fucking money."

"And if he comes back but he ain't got all of your bread then what?"

"Y'all niggas are shooters. That means you just got a fucking job working for me. I can always use a shooter."

Jamaica didn't say anything, he just looked at Killer when there was a knock at the door.

Animal watched Killer go to the door and open it.

That's when Savage walked into the apartment up to Animal. He looked at Jamaica. "You good, family?"

"Yeah, I'm 100 dog."

"Don't worry if that nigga is good or not. You got my fucking money?"

"Yeah, I got your money." Savage pulled off the bookbag and passed it to Animal.

Animal looked inside and saw all the money. "Yo, Killer, it ain't even been 48 hours and this little nigga brought me the bag. Yo, go count this money and make sure it's all there." Animal passed the bookbag to Killer then looked back at Savage. Killer walked off to the back. "Where you get that money from?"

"Does it matter as long as you get paid?"

"You know what? If you wasn't such a real nigga, I would body your ass. It's just… it's hard being a real nigga and you are standing ten toes down on it."

Savage ain't say shit, he just looked at Animal smoke his cigar as Killer walked back up on them.

"It's all there, down to the last penny."

Animal nodded. "I'ma let you two niggas walk the fuck up out of here. But next time you fuck with my shit, that magic bitch ain't going back in that bottle. Killer, show these two little niggas the door."

Savage and Jamaica walked out of the apartment.

Jamaica looked at Savage. "Yo, how the fuck you come up with that bread that fast, homie?"

"Come on. I'll tell you when we get into the car, fam." Savage kept looking over his shoulder as they made it to the car to make sure nobody was following them.

Once in the car, Jamaica looked at Tasha as she pulled off.

"Jamaica, this is my fam Tasha. She was the one who helped me get the money up to get you up out of there."

"Good looking, ma. That shit was ugly. I just knew them niggas was going to roll me."

"It was because of us you got put in that situation so we had to stay ten toes down and get you the fuck up out of there."

"That's respect and love, Tasha."
Tasha just nodded, not saying nothing else.

***

Nicole was watching the news. She couldn't believe what she was hearing. Someone killed Style-B at his apartment. She was just there with him not even 6 hours ago. She'd only been talking to him for a few weeks but she really did like him. She had tears in her eyes just thinking about the last time they were together, how they had a fight over a picture that was sent to his phone. She wished she could turn back the hands of time. She got up and walked outside to her car. She had to go see this for herself with her own two eyes.

Chapter 45

"Yo, Ray-J, I see you really been caked up lately. Let me find out you in love, nigga."

Ray-J pulled the blunt and looked at Rip. "Hell naw, dog. I'm just fucking with this bad bitch I met a few weeks ago."

"You fuck her yet?"

"Not yet but I'm on my way there. We are supposed to link up later tonight when she leaves the studio."

"Owe, you got yourself a little rapping bitch."

"Real talk, she just started going to the studio, but she got a nice little flow."

"Wait, you linking up with her tonight?"

"Yeah."

"Don't you got to make them drop-offs for Cash?"

"Damn, I forgot about that shit. I'ma take care of the business though."

"Don't let that pussy get you fucked up, bro. You know every time a nigga fall victim, it's over a bitch. Just think about that."

"Listen, man. I ain't no pussy-whipped ass nigga. I break the bitch; I don't let the bitch break me."

"Say less, pimp. I hear you." Rip started laughing as he got up and gave Ray-J a pound before walking out the trap house.

Ray-J stuck up his middle finger at Rip as he walked out the door then went back to texting Tasha.

***

"Tasha, you ready for tonight?" Gangstar asked her as he was cleaning his gun.

"Yeah, I'm ready."

"Good, because tonight this nigga Ray-J is going to see his maker. It's time we start bodying these Brown niggas one by-fucking-one."

Gangstar didn't know that Tasha's heart already started to get cold with Wolf being the first person that she had a part of killing. And with her killing Style-B, shit started to get real dark to her, and the only person she started to give a fuck about was herself— no one else. Gangstar was her dude, but he wasn't even after the bag no more; just revenge on Cash, and he ain't even see that he was still losing. She just got up and went to the room, not saying nothing. She had to get ready for tonight.

***

Ray-J stepped out of his car. He lowered his head to light his blunt before he walked into the studio. The music was blasting real loud; he was bumping his head to the music. He saw Tasha's little cute ass. He loved her hourglass shape and her brown skin tone. It'd been a few weeks they'd been talking and he promised himself he was going to fuck her tonight. He watched as she was flowing. She had a flow like Remy Ma and was running neck to neck with Cardi-B, with her sexy ass. She saw Ray-J smoking the blunt. She smiled, put the mic down, and walked up to him and kissed him on the lips.

"I see you in here doing your thing, sexy."

"You know I be dropping them bars when I'm in the booth."

"Already, but I got some shit to do. So, you ready, sexy?"

161

"Yeah, I'm ready, but I'm hungry. So, can we stop at Uncle's Grill on the way out before you go take care of your business?"

"Yeah, we can do that. I got some time to kill." Ray-J hugged Tasha as they walked out of the studio to his car. He threw his blunt on the ground as he opened the door for Tasha to get inside. "So, how was the studio session today?"

"That shit was lit-lit. I think I got my first hit for the radio."

"Word? I can't wait to hear it."

"I got you, daddy."

"So, what you trying to eat from Uncle's Grill?"

"I want the family plate. Mac and Cheese, baked sweet bread, his famous ribs that just fall off the bone, and that apple pie."

"Damn, you trying to be a fat girl?"

"Whatever, I'm trying to eat."

Ray-J smiled. As he pulled into the parking lot of Uncle's Grill, he cut his car off and looked at Tasha.

"Bae, I'll be right out. You want something?"

"No, I'm good. just hurry your sexy ass up. I got some moves to make."

"Don't worry, daddy. I'll be fast." Tasha stepped out of the car and looked to the right at the black Escalade that was parked there.

That's when the door opened and Gangstar stepped out wearing all black. He ran up to the side of Ray-J's car and with the butt of the gun smashed the window out. He pointed the gun at Ray-J's face.

Ray-J was lost for words as he looked at the gun in his face.

"Yeah, nigga! It's me, Gangstar, motherfucker! You know it's beef any time I see one of you niggas on the street. This beef is just getting started, pussy! Go-Getters for life," was all that Ray-J heard as the sound of the Glock-40 unloaded into his chest, killing him and the echoing of the gun blast was all you heard in the parking lot.

Ray-J laid there with five bullet holes in his chest, dead with his eyes open with tears rolling out of them.

Gangstar ran back to the SUV and looked at Tasha on the passenger side of the Escalade. She waited for him to drive off. She leaned over and kissed him. As he was pulling out of the parking lot, people were running out to see what was going on. Then they saw Ray-J's dead body shot up in the car with blood dripping from his mouth

***

Damn. Like I said in the beginning when Tigger killed KP, I knew it was going to be a bloody summer and that bodies were going to drop. When Cash told me I better paint the walls, the inside of the car, the sidewalks with Tigger's blood, and if the police is there I better crash out, I knew I had to stand on business because so much depends on our reputation. We kill niggas because we build it with our lives. I knew the way I killed Tigger that my karma was going to come back on me, but I ain't know my summer was going to end like this with me trying to catch my breath with tears in my eyes. I guess in the end it really doesn't matter what side you are on. B-God, SB, KP were all my homies. Even Gangstar had homies. Showtime, Tigger, Killer-B. We all ended up the same way. Trying to catch our breath with tears in our eyes. I guess at the end of the day, no matter what side you are on, when them bullets hit you, you can't stop them tears from coming to your eyes. I guess that's the meaning of **opps cry too**.

To be continued…

Lock Down Publications and Ca$h Presents Assisted Publishing Packages

Due to an increase in the price of services we have increased our prices. The prices below reflect the price increase as of 11/1/24.

BASIC PACKAGE	UPGRADED PACKAGE
$699 Editing Cover Design Formatting	**$1000** Typing Editing Cover Design Formatting Upload eBooks to Amazon Upload Paperback to Amazon
ADVANCE PACKAGE **$1,400** Typing Editing (line editing/content) Cover Design Formatting Copyright Registration Proofreading Upload eBooks to Amazon Upload Paperback to Amazon	**LDP SUPREME PACKAGE** **$1,700** Typing Editing (line editing/content) Cover Design Formatting Copyright Registration Proofreading Set up Amazon Account Upload eBooks to Amazon Upload Paperback to Amazon Advertise on LDP's Amazon and Facebook Page

***Other services available upon request.
Additional charges may apply

Lock Down Publications
P.O. Box 944
Stockbridge, GA 30281-9998
Phone: 470 303-9761
Email: lockdownpublications@gmail.com

Submission Guideline

Submit the first three chapters of your completed manuscript to ldpsubmissions@gmail.com. In the subject line add **Your Book's Title**. The manuscript must be in a Word Doc file and sent as an attachment. Document should be in Times New Roman, double spaced, and in size 12 font. Also, provide your synopsis and full contact information. If sending multiple submissions, they must each be in a separate email.

Have a story but no way to send it electronically? You can still submit to LDP/Ca$h Presents. Send in the first three chapters, written or typed, of your completed manuscript to:

LDP: Submissions Dept
P.O. Box 944
Stockbridge, GA 30281-9998

DO NOT send original manuscript. Must be a duplicate. Provide your synopsis and a cover letter containing your full contact information.

Thanks for considering LDP and Ca$h Presents.

NEW RELEASES

BLOODLINE OF A SAVAGE 1&2
THESE VICIOUS STREETS 1&2
RELENTLESS GOON
RELENTLESS GOON 2
BY PRINCE A. TAUHID

THE BUTTERFLY MAFIA 1-3
BY FUMIYA PAYNE

A THUG'S STREET PRINCESS 1&2
BY MEESHA

CITY OF SMOKE 2
BY MOLOTTI

STEPPERS 1,2&3
THE REAL BADDIES OF CHI-RAQ
BY KING RIO

THE LANE 1&2
BY KEN-KEN SPENCE

THUG OF SPADES 1&2
LOVE IN THE TRENCHES 2
CORNER BOYS
BY COREY ROBINSON

TIL DEATH 3
BY ARYANNA

THE BIRTH OF A GANGSTER 4
BY DELMONT PLAYER

PRODUCT OF THE STREETS 1&2
BY DEMOND "MONEY" ANDERSON

NO TIME FOR ERROR
BY KEESE

MONEY HUNGRY DEMONS
BY TRANAY ADAMS

Coming Soon from Lock Down Publications/Ca$h Presents

IF YOU CROSS ME ONCE 6
ANGEL V
By Anthony Fields

IMMA DIE BOUT MINE 5
By Aryanna

A THUGS STREET PRINCESS 3
By Meesha

PRODUCT OF THE STREETS 3
By Demond Money Anderson

CORNER BOYS 2
By Corey Robinson

THE MURDER QUEENS 6&7
By Michael Gallon

CITY OF SMOKE 3
By Molotti

CONFESSIONS OF A DOPE BOY
By Nicholas Lock

THA TAKEOVER
By Keith Chandler

BETRAYAL OF A G 2
By Ray Vinci

CRIME BOSS
By Playa Ray

Available Now

RESTRAINING ORDER 1 & 2
By **CA$H & Coffee**

LOVE KNOWS NO BOUNDARIES 1-3
By **Coffee**

RAISED AS A GOON I, II, III & IV
BRED BY THE SLUMS I, II, III
BLAST FOR ME I & II
ROTTEN TO THE CORE I II III
A BRONX TALE I, II, III
DUFFLE BAG CARTEL I II III IV V VI
HEARTLESS GOON I II III IV V
A SAVAGE DOPEBOY I II
DRUG LORDS I II III
CUTTHROAT MAFIA I II
KING OF THE TRENCHES
By **Ghost**

LAY IT DOWN I & II
LAST OF A DYING BREED I II
BLOOD STAINS OF A SHOTTA I & II III
By **Jamaica**

LOYAL TO THE GAME I II III
LIFE OF SIN I, II III
By **TJ & Jelissa**

IF LOVING HIM IS WRONG…I & II
LOVE ME EVEN WHEN IT HURTS I II III
By **Jelissa**

PUSH IT TO THE LIMIT
By **Bre' Hayes**

BLOODY COMMAS I & II
SKI MASK CARTEL I, II & III
KING OF NEW YORK I II, III IV V
RISE TO POWER I II III
COKE KINGS I II III IV V
BORN HEARTLESS I II III IV
KING OF THE TRAP I II
By **T.J. Edwards**

WHEN THE STREETS CLAP BACK I & II III
THE HEART OF A SAVAGE I II III IV
MONEY MAFIA I II
LOYAL TO THE SOIL I II III
By **Jibril Williams**

A DISTINGUISHED THUG STOLE MY HEART I II & III
LOVE SHOULDN'T HURT I II III IV
RENEGADE BOYS 1-4
PAID IN KARMA 1-3
SAVAGE STORMS 1-3
AN UNFORESEEN LOVE 1-3
BABY, I'M WINTERTIME COLD 1-3
A THUG'S STREET PRINCESS 1&2
By **Meesha**

A GANGSTER'S CODE 1-3
A GANGSTER'S SYN 1-3
THE SAVAGE LIFE 1-3
CHAINED TO THE STREETS 1-3
BLOOD ON THE MONEY 1-3
A GANGSTA'S PAIN 1-3
BEAUTIFUL LIES AND UGLY TRUTHS
CHURCH IN THESE STREETS
By **J-Blunt**

CUM FOR ME 1-8
An LDP Erotica Collaboration

BLOOD OF A BOSS 1-5
SHADOWS OF THE GAME
TRAP BASTARD
By **Askari**

THE STREETS BLEED MURDER 1-3
THE HEART OF A GANGSTA 1-3
By **Jerry Jackson**

WHEN A GOOD GIRL GOES BAD
By **Adrienne**

THE COST OF LOYALTY 1-3
By **Kweli**

BRIDE OF A HUSTLA 1-3
THE FETTI GIRLS 1-3
CORRUPTED BY A GANGSTA 1-4
BLINDED BY HIS LOVE
THE PRICE YOU PAY FOR LOVE 1-3
DOPE GIRL MAGIC 1-3
By **Destiny Skai**

A KINGPIN'S AMBITION
A KINGPIN'S AMBITION II
I MURDER FOR THE DOUGH
By **Ambitious**

TRUE SAVAGE 1-7
DOPE BOY MAGIC 1-3
MIDNIGHT CARTEL 1-3
CITY OF KINGZ 1&2
NIGHTMARE ON SILENT AVE
THE PLUG OF LIL MEXICO 1&2
CLASSIC CITY
By **Chris Green**

A GANGSTER'S REVENGE 1-4
THE BOSS MAN'S DAUGHTERS 1-5
A SAVAGE LOVE 1&2
BAE BELONGS TO ME 1&2
A HUSTLER'S DECEIT 1-3
WHAT BAD BITCHES DO 1-3
SOUL OF A MONSTER 1-3
KILL ZONE
A DOPE BOY'S QUEEN 1-3
TIL DEATH 1-3
IMMA DIE BOUT MINE 1-4
By **Aryanna**

A DOPEBOY'S PRAYER
By **Eddie "Wolf" Lee**

THE KING CARTEL 1-3
By **Frank Gresham**

THESE NIGGAS AIN'T LOYAL 1-3
By **Nikki Tee**

GANGSTA SHYT 1-3
By **CATO**

THE ULTIMATE BETRAYAL
By **Phoenix**

BOSS'N UP 1-3
By **Royal Nicole**

I LOVE YOU TO DEATH
By **Destiny J**

I RIDE FOR MY HITTA
I STILL RIDE FOR MY HITTA
By **Misty Holt**

LOVE & CHASIN' PAPER
By **Qay Crockett**

TO DIE IN VAIN
SINS OF A HUSTLA
By **ASAD**

BROOKLYN HUSTLAZ
By **Boogsy Morina**

BROOKLYN ON LOCK 1 & 2
By **Sonovia**

GANGSTA CITY
By **Teddy Duke**

A DRUG KING AND HIS DIAMOND 1-3
A DOPEMAN'S RICHES
HER MAN, MINE'S TOO 1&2
CASH MONEY HO'S
THE WIFEY I USED TO BE 1&2
PRETTY GIRLS DO NASTY THINGS
By **Nicole Goosby**

LIPSTICK KILLAH 1-3
CRIME OF PASSION 1-3
FRIEND OR FOE 1-3
By **Mimi**

TRAPHOUSE KING 1-3
KINGPIN KILLAZ 1-3
STREET KINGS 1&2
PAID IN BLOOD 1&2
CARTEL KILLAZ 1-3
DOPE GODS 1&2
By **Hood Rich**

THE STREETS ARE CALLING
By **Duquie Wilson**

STEADY MOBBN' 1-3
THE STREETS STAINED MY SOUL 1-3
By **Marcellus Allen**

WHO SHOT YA 1-3
SON OF A DOPE FIEND 1-4
HEAVEN GOT A GHETTO 1&2
SKI MASK MONEY 1&2
By **Renta**

GORILLAZ IN THE BAY 1-4
TEARS OF A GANGSTA 1/&2
3X KRAZY 1&2
STRAIGHT BEAST MODE 1&2
By **DE'KARI**

TRIGGADALE 1-3
MURDA WAS THE CASE 1-3
By **Elijah R. Freeman**

SLAUGHTER GANG 1-3
RUTHLESS HEART 1-3
By **Willie Slaughter**

GOD BLESS THE TRAPPERS 1-3
THESE SCANDALOUS STREETS 1-3
FEAR MY GANGSTA 1-5
THESE STREETS DON'T LOVE NOBODY 1-2
BURY ME A G 1-5
A GANGSTA'S EMPIRE 1-4
THE DOPEMAN'S BODYGAURD 1&2
THE REALEST KILLAZ 1-3
THE LAST OF THE OGS 1-3
By **Tranay Adams**

MARRIED TO A BOSS 1-3
By **Destiny Skai & Chris Green**

KINGZ OF THE GAME 1-7
CRIME BOSS 1-3
By **Playa Ray**

FUK SHYT
By **Blakk Diamond**

DON'T F#CK WITH MY HEART 1&2
By **Linnea**

ADDICTED TO THE DRAMA 1-3
IN THE ARM OF HIS BOSS
By **Jamila**

LOYALTY AIN'T PROMISED 1&2
By **Keith Williams**

YAYO 1-4
A SHOOTER'S AMBITION 1&2
BRED IN THE GAME
By **S. Allen**

TRAP GOD 1-3
RICH $AVAGE 1-3
MONEY IN THE GRAVE 1-3
CARTEL MONEY
By **Martell Troublesome Bolden**

FOREVER GANGSTA 1&2
GLOCKS ON SATIN SHEETS 1&2
By **Adrian Dulan**

TOE TAGZ 1-4
LEVELS TO THIS SHYT 1&2
IT'S JUST ME AND YOU
By **Ah'Million**

OPPS CRY TOO | SAYNOMORE

KINGPIN DREAMS 1-3
RAN OFF ON DA PLUG
By **Paper Boi Rari**

THE STREETS MADE ME 1-3
By **Larry D. Wright**

CONFESSIONS OF A GANGSTA 1-4
CONFESSIONS OF A JACKBOY 1-3
CONFESSIONS OF A HITMAN
By **Nicholas Lock**

I'M NOTHING WITHOUT HIS LOVE
SINS OF A THUG
TO THE THUG I LOVED BEFORE
A GANGSTA SAVED XMAS
IN A HUSTLER I TRUST
By **Monet Dragun**

QUIET MONEY 1-3
THUG LIFE 1-3
EXTENDED CLIP 1&2
A GANGSTA'S PARADISE
By **Trai'Quan**

CAUGHT UP IN THE LIFE 1-3
THE STREETS NEVER LET GO 1-3
By **Robert Baptiste**

NEW TO THE GAME 1-3
MONEY, MURDER & MEMORIES 1-3
By **Malik D. Rice**

CREAM 2-3
THE STREETS WILL TALK
By **Yolanda Moore**

THE STREETS WILL NEVER CLOSE 1-3
By **K'ajji**

LIFE OF A SAVAGE 1-4
A GANGSTA'S QUR'AN 1-4
MURDA SEASON 1-3
GANGLAND CARTEL 1-3
CHI'RAQ GANGSTAS 1-4
KILLERS ON ELM STREET 1-3
JACK BOYZ N DA BRONX 1-3
A DOPEBOY'S DREAM 1-3
JACK BOYS VS DOPE BOYS 1-3
COKE GIRLZ
COKE BOYS
SOSA GANG 1&2
BRONX SAVAGES
BODYMORE KINGPINS
BLOOD OF A GOON
By **Romell Tukes**

CONCRETE KILLA 1-3
VICIOUS LOYALTY 1-3
By **Kingpen**

THE ULTIMATE SACRIFICE 1-6
KHADIFI
IF YOU CROSS ME ONCE 1-3
ANGEL 1-4
IN THE BLINK OF AN EYE
By **Anthony Fields**

THE LIFE OF A HOOD STAR
By **Ca$h & Rashia Wilson**

NIGHTMARES OF A HUSTLA 1-3
BLOOD AND GAMES 1&2
By **King Dream**

GHOST MOB
By **Stilloan Robinson**

HARD AND RUTHLESS 1&2
MOB TOWN 251
THE BILLIONAIRE BENTLEYS 1-3
REAL G'S MOVE IN SILENCE
By **Von Diesel**

MOB TIES 1-7
SOUL OF A HUSTLER, HEART OF A KILLER 1-3
GORILLAZ IN THE TRENCHES
By **SayNoMore**

BODYMORE MURDERLAND 1-3
THE BIRTH OF A GANGSTER 1-4
By **Delmont Player**

FOR THE LOVE OF A BOSS 1&2
By **C. D. Blue**

KILLA KOUNTY 1-5
By **Khufu**

MOBBED UP 1-4
THE BRICK MAN 1-5
THE COCAINE PRINCESS 1-10
STEPPERS 1-3
SUPER GREMLIN 1-4
By **King Rio**

MONEY GAME 1&2
By **Smoove Dolla**

A GANGSTA'S KARMA 1-4
By **FLAME**

KING OF THE TRENCHES 1-3
By **GHOST & TRANAY ADAMS**

OPPS CRY TOO | SAYNOMORE

QUEEN OF THE ZOO 1&2
By **Black Migo**

GRIMEY WAYS 1-3
BETRAYAL OF A G
By **Ray Vinci**

XMAS WITH AN ATL SHOOTER
By **Ca$h & Destiny Skai**

KING KILLA 1&2
By **Vincent "Vitto" Holloway**

BETRAYAL OF A THUG 1&2
By **Fre$h**

THE MURDER QUEENS 1-5
By **Michael Gallon**

FOR THE LOVE OF BLOOD 1-4
By **Jamel Mitchell**

HOOD CONSIGLIERE 1&2
NO TIME FOR ERROR
By **Keese**

PROTÉGÉ OF A LEGEND 1&2
LOVE IN THE TRENCHES 1&2
By **Corey Robinson**

THE PLUG'S RUTHLESS DAUGHTER
By **Tony Daniels**

BORN IN THE GRAVE 1-3
CRIME PAYS
By **Self Made Tay**

MOAN IN MY MOUTH
By **XTASY**

TORN BETWEEN A GANGSTER AND A GENTLEMAN
By **J-BLUNT & Miss Kim**

LOYALTY IS EVERYTHING 1-3
CITY OF SMOKE 1&2
By **Molotti**

HERE TODAY GONE TOMORROW 1&2
By **Fly Rock**

WOMEN LIE MEN LIE 1-4
FIFTY SHADES OF SNOW 1-3
STACK BEFORE YOU SPLURGE
GIRLS FALL LIKE DOMINOES
NAÏVE TO THE STREETS
By **ROY MILLIGAN**

PILLOW PRINCESS
By **S. Hawkins**

THE BUTTERFLY MAFIA 1-3
SALUTE MY SAVAGERY 1&2
By **Fumiya Payne**

THE LANE 1&2
By Ken-Ken Spence

THE PUSSY TRAP 1-5
By **Nene Capri**

DIRTY DNA
By **Blaque**

SANCTIFIED AND HORNY
by **XTASY**

BOOKS BY LDP'S CEO, CA$H

TRUST IN NO MAN
TRUST IN NO MAN 2
TRUST IN NO MAN 3
BONDED BY BLOOD
SHORTY GOT A THUG
THUGS CRY
THUGS CRY 2
THUGS CRY 3
TRUST NO BITCH
TRUST NO BITCH 2
TRUST NO BITCH 3
TIL MY CASKET DROPS
RESTRAINING ORDER
RESTRAINING ORDER 2
IN LOVE WITH A CONVICT
LIFE OF A HOOD STAR
XMAS WITH AN ATL SHOOTER

www.ingramcontent.com/pod-product-compliance
Lightning Source LLC
Chambersburg PA
CBHW070524260626
47161CB00004B/1629

* 9 7 8 1 9 6 5 4 4 8 3 3 5 *